MW00440412

SPELLBOUND

SWEETS

Connie Shelton

Books by Connie Shelton

THE CHARLIE PARKER MYSTERY SERIES

Deadly Gamble
Vacations Can Be Murder
Partnerships Can Be Murder
Small Towns Can Be Murder
Memories Can Be Murder
Honeymoons Can Be Murder
Reunions Can Be Murder
Competition Can Be Murder
Balloons Can Be Murder
Obsessions Can Be Murder
Gossip Can Be Murder
Stardom Can Be Murder
Phantoms Can Be Murder
Buried Secrets Can Be Murder
Legends Can Be Murder
Weddings Can Be Murder
Holidays Can Be Murder - a Christmas novella

THE SAMANTHA SWEET MYSTERY SERIES

Sweet Masterpiece
Sweet's Sweets
Sweet Holidays
Sweet Hearts
Bitter Sweet
Sweets Galore
Sweets Begorra
Sweet Payback
Sweet Somethings
Sweets Forgotten
Spooky Sweet
The Woodcarver's Secret
Spellbound Sweets - a Halloween novella

THE HEIST LADIES SERIES

Diamonds Aren't Forever
The Trophy Wife Exchange

CHILDREN'S BOOKS

Daisy and Maisie and the Great Lizard Hunt
Daisy and Maisie and the Lost Kitten

SPELLBOUND SWEETS

A Samantha Sweet Halloween Novella

Connie Shelton

Secret Staircase Books

Spellbound Sweets
Published by Secret Staircase Books, an imprint of
Columbine Publishing Group
PO Box 416, Angel Fire, NM 87710

Book layout and design by Secret Staircase Books

First trade paperback edition: October 2017
First e-book editions: September 2016
(included in the collection, *Midnight Mysteries*)

Publisher's Cataloging-in-Publication Data

Shelton, Connie
Spellbound Sweets / by Connie Shelton
p. cm.
ISBN 978-1945422331 (paperback)

1. Sweet, Samantha (Fictitious character)--Fiction. 2. Women
sleuths--Fiction. 3. Taos, New Mexico--Fiction. 4. Paranormal
artifacts--Fiction. 5. Chocolate making--Fiction.
6. Halloween--Fiction. I. Title

Samantha Sweet Mystery Series : Halloween novella
Shelton, Connie, Samantha Sweet mysteries.

BISAC : FICTION / Mystery & Detective / Cozy.
813/.54

To all my readers who brighten my day with your sweet comments. The fact that you love my stories and characters makes it all worthwhile.

A huge thank-you, as always, to my editorial team. Susan Slater and Shirley Shaw, you keep my writing on track. Ritter Ames, thanks so much for suggesting I write this Halloween novella in the first place, and for including my work in the same collection with all the other talented writers in Midnight Mysteries!

Chapter 1

Samantha Sweet felt her smile stiffen and she attempted to conceal her impatience from her customer. They sat at one of the two-place bistro tables in her shop, going over design ideas for a wedding cake.

"But classic black is what I *want*," whined Cassie Wolinsky, the bride. "It's Halloween, I'm a witch, we wear black. The cake should be black too."

"The cake *and* the icing?" Sam asked. "Not chocolate. Black."

"Yes! Exactly!"

A stiff breeze fluttered the awnings above the display windows at Sweet's Sweets, and a deep rumble of thunder sidetracked Sam's attention momentarily. She re-focused on her pencil and the order form before her, sketching what she thought Cassie wanted. Four tiers of sponge cake, which would have to be tinted with heavy doses of pure black food coloring. The bottom tier would be shaped as a thick book of spells with magical sparkles wafting upward across the other tiers. Miss Wolinsky's other elements must include a black hat, a black magic wand, some black potion bottles and a black cat. The challenge for the bakery team would be to make the black-on-black objects stand out. She had a vision of the whole thing ending up a huge lumpy-looking dark mass.

"It might be nice to have another color to help offset some of these," she suggested, trying not to reveal her thoughts—that the idea was just plain weird. "If the magic sparkles are silver or gold—"

"Well, *yeah*, they have to be silver," Cassie said, as if any dunce would know.

"So ... how about if we use silver for the potion bottles too? And maybe the wand?" The piece was feeling more like a theme cake for a kid's birthday than a wedding cake. The idea bothered Sam more than it should.

Cassie's eyes, directed toward the ceiling, told Sam how little the bride thought of the idea. "See, this is exactly why I didn't bring my *mother* with me. You're just not getting it."

Okay, I'm sure I'm old enough to be your mother, but don't give me the eye-roll, young lady. Sheesh! Sam caught herself. Normally, she loved hearing her customers' innovative ideas, and the challenge of turning their dreams into beautiful pastries was what Sweet's Sweets bake shop was all about.

She'd simply been working too many late nights recently. Halloween being one of their major busy times, up there with Christmas, Valentine's Day and the wedding season, the extra hours were to be expected. Face it, as owner of the premier one-of-a-kind pastry shop in Taos she'd brought this upon herself.

Jennifer Baca, Sam's assistant who worked behind the counter and often took custom orders as well, spoke up: "I went to a wedding in Albuquerque last month where the couple chose a steampunk theme. Come to think of it, their cake was almost completely black. Maybe I can help with this one?"

The bride seemed inordinately relieved at this suggestion, more so when Jen took over the sketchpad. Within fifteen minutes they had a drawing to work from, a cash deposit (which Sam couldn't belittle—it had turned out to be quite an expensive cake), and Cass, as Jen now called her, happily left to climb into her black and silver Mini Cooper parked outside. She'd no sooner started the car than the storm intensified. A bolt of lightning flashed, blazing across the front windows and making Sam jump. Rain pelted the sidewalk.

Once they were alone again she thanked Jen for coming to her rescue. "I'm not the ancient crone she thinks I am. Really. Fifty-four is hardly decrepit."

Jen, who had been Sam's daughter's friend in high school, put an arm around Sam's shoulders in a quick hug. "You? Not a bit. If fifty is the new thirty, then *you* are about eighteen. I've never met anyone with your energy."

Sam thought about the real cause for most of her energy binges, a mysterious carved wooden box she'd received a few years ago. She and the box had made some kind of magical connection—the way an electrical zing charged through her body the first time she touched it, the fact that she sometimes saw auras now, the healing touch she had applied to injuries on several occasions. Sam couldn't explain it, and no one other than her dear husband Beau knew it. A few suspected, and a couple of close encounters with some dangerous people had convinced her the box must remain secret.

She shook off those thoughts. She hadn't used the box's powers in months and although it would have made the holiday season much easier to handle, she was determined to make it through on her own stamina. Just a few more nights to work late and she could take a few days off before the Thanksgiving pie orders began to flow in.

"I like it," Jen said, studying the black wedding cake sketch. "If the steampunk one I saw can provide a clue, it seemed to include very small variations in the depth of the black color. You know, a little less for the background, a bit more for the lace and flounces … think of it as fifty shades of black."

Sam nodded. She and her decorator would have to put their heads together on this one. It still posed a challenge. She was heading to the kitchen to show the order to Becky when the bells at the front door tinkled and the owner of Mysterious Happenings, the bookshop next door, breezed in.

"Good morning, lovely ladies! I am coming over to be inviting you to a party." Ivan Petrenko was always cheerful and usually over-the-top with his compliments, although his curious accent and fractured English sometimes took a moment to decipher. "Is for Halloween, the party, and we must all dress."

Jen giggled. "Maybe you mean dress up?"

"*Oui*, of course. What do you think I say? We dress like the characters from mystery books." He turned to Sam with his quirky smile. "There must be dessert. I will leave to your capable hands. Your friend Rupert is making the entertainment. All the bakery must come. Your beautiful daughter shall come, your husband—but tell him no wearing uniform, must be a book character. *Da?*"

"I'll see what I can do," Sam promised. "*Da. Ja ... oui* ... whatever."

"*Spasibo!*" With that, he bustled out the door and headed back to his shop.

"Thanks?" Jen guessed. "So, did he once tell me he escaped Soviet Russia and lived in various parts of Europe before coming here?"

Sam nodded. "That's the story. He does seem to have quite the multicultural manner, doesn't he?"

She carried the witchy wedding cake design to the kitchen, her mind already flitting between what type of dessert she could make for Ivan's party and how on earth she would convince the county sheriff to dress up as a literary character.

Chapter 2

Ugh, Sam, you know I hate that stuff," Beau said when she told him about the costume party later at home.

She had grilled steaks and made a colorful salad, hoping to turn his mood in favor of the idea. Her handsome husband could be spontaneous and fun-loving—she still remembered their first date where they ate his homemade chili and watched the sunset—but costumes just weren't his thing.

"I know, but I told Ivan I would ask."

"If you *really* want to do it, and *if* I'm not working that night …" He cut a bite of his steak and began chewing, making it seem as if he'd been just about ready to agree but didn't quite get the words out.

"You'll be working," she said with a grin. "It happens

every year because Halloween is one of the weirdest nights of the year for pranks and parties and drunks …" Even small towns weren't immune.

"It is. And there's a full moon this year. I checked. The department will be crazy-busy."

She laughed at the vision that popped into her head. Werewolf costumes would surely abound. "It's fine, hon. I'll go because he's a neighbor and because he sends so much business my way. The party is officially being hosted by his Chocoholics Unanimous book group and they are a fun bunch. It's a mystery theme and Rupert is apparently writing some kind of little play or skit for entertainment. He was pretty cagey when I called him. I'm trying to come up with something unique to make for their dessert so I thought I could use the theme of his play. He would only say that he found a cool old book in a flea market stall and is building a story around it."

"Well, I'm sure everyone will have a great time," Beau said as he forked up a big bite of his baked potato. "What's your costume going to be?"

"I have no idea. It's another addition to my to-do list, which is already long enough this week, as it is."

"You will manage brilliantly, as you always do." He planted a kiss on the top of her short gray hair and began clearing the table.

While he loaded the dishwasher, Sam searched for a scratchpad. With the party and now a costume to figure out, she'd better make some notes. All the mystery characters who came to mind seemed clichéd and overdone. She was hardly the Sherlock Holmes type, and a woman her age with a chunky build didn't exactly fit the Nancy Drew persona. Although she would never be model-gorgeous,

Beau was a very attractive man. If she could get him to commit to the party they might consider being a couple such as Nick and Nora Charles or the TV guy, Castle, and that cop who became his romantic interest. She scratched through those names. There was a ninety percent chance Beau would not be able to go, even if she could convince him he wanted to. Plus, she could never pull off the image. The empty page stared at her. She reached for her phone and called her best friend.

"I need costume ideas," Sam moaned.

"If it's for Ivan's party, I can tell you a couple that have already been taken. I'm proud to say Rupert asked me to be the leading lady in his play and I'll be going as a witch." Zoë, a sort of flower-child holdover from the '60s, with her wavy gray, shoulder-length hair could easily pull off that role.

"A witch? What literary character is that?"

"Well, if anyone asks, I'm Glinda the Good Witch of the North. For the play, I don't think it matters."

"What's the play about?"

"Um, I'm not supposed to say."

"Zoë ... come on."

"I haven't seen the script. All I know is that he's using some old book of spells and I'll need to recite one of them."

"Double, double, toil and trouble?"

Zoë's chipper laugh came through loud and clear. "Most likely, something like that."

"So, you aren't going to feed me a brilliant idea for a costume, are you?"

"Sweetie, I would but I'm fresh out. Plus, we have guests walking through the front door right now and I need to show them to their rooms. Gotta go."

Sam felt her mouth twist into a peevish wrinkle. Between Zoë and Darryl's bed and breakfast and her own bakery she and her friend didn't get nearly enough time to simply kick back and laugh over things the way they used to. She set the notepad aside and went to the kitchen for a cup of tea.

Beau had left the kitchen spotless, bless him. She could hear his voice out on the porch as he set bowls down for their two dogs, Ranger and Nellie. No doubt he would next head for the barn to check on the horses and lock up for the night. The ranch property on the outskirts of Taos was their little haven of peace and quiet, and Sam loved the break it gave her from the bakery. Animals and property meant extra work, though, and she was lucky Beau enjoyed it enough to handle nearly everything. She brewed two cups of tea and walked out to the deck in time to catch him on his way back from the barn. The afternoon storm had moved out swiftly. Overhead, the sky showed off the glittering swath of the Milky Way. They sank onto their favorite deck chairs with their mugs until the high-desert chill of a late October night sent them back indoors.

Sam fell asleep with no great ideas for a Halloween costume and with the decision about a dessert for the party crowd hanging over her.

When her alarm went off at four-thirty she popped out of bed without hesitation. She'd had a silly dream about Cass Wolinsky's wedding—the young witch bride, dressed in black, practically disappearing behind her all-black cake when the photographer tried to frame acceptable pictures. The scene caught in Sam's head as she awoke and she knew just what dessert to make for Ivan's party.

Chapter 3

Julio Ortiz was already at work when Sam arrived, producing the standard breakfast pastries to fill the shelves for the morning crowd. This time of year, the offerings included lots of apples and spice—muffins, scones, and their seasonal favorite, a caramel-pear cheesecake. He pulled a rack of cinnamon streusel-topped muffins from the oven as Sam removed her coat.

"Wow—you would think I'd be immune by now," she said, "but that scent always makes my knees weak."

He sent a rare smile her way. Despite his rough appearance, tattooed arms, taciturn manner and the Harley parked out back, Julio was the best treasure she'd ever found for her business. The man knew his way around a kitchen and worked without comment or complaint, day in and day out.

"When you get the next batch into the oven and you have a minute, let's talk about an odd order I took yesterday."

She walked to the back of the room to hang up her coat and wash her hands. When she turned around Julio was waiting beside the large stainless steel worktable in the middle of the kitchen. She showed him the drawing for the black wedding cake and her suggestion to the bride that they would tint regular sponge cake to the right intensity.

"I'll get more black food color on order right away. We'll be going through a lot of it this week."

He nodded and pulled out pans for the layer sizes she needed.

She placed the online supply order with next-day delivery before pulling out her pastry bags and decorating tips. She had piped ghostly shapes and spooky black eyes on the tops of two dozen cupcakes, frosted four dozen orange pumpkin cookies, and added little green goblins to a panful of brownies by the time the rest of the staff arrived. Although the whole crew consisted only of Jen, Becky and Julio, Sam called a little meeting.

"It's going to be a busy week," she said. "You all know how the holidays are—we've done this every year. Jen may have told you, there's a treat at the end of all the hard work this time, the party at the bookstore Saturday night."

Becky's face lit up and she exchanged a look with Jen. Julio might have grumbled down low in his throat.

"We're making the dessert—Chocoholics theme. Becky, I'll talk details with you later. Meanwhile, you all can be thinking about costumes and whether you want to bring a date. Just don't let party plans distract you too much. We also have to get eighteen dozen cupcakes ready for various school moms, four birthday theme cakes, and a black wedding in addition to a couple of more traditional ones. And that's just the Halloween items. We still have all the usual."

The oven timer punctuated that last statement, reminding Julio to take his cheesecake out of the oven, and the front doorbell called out to Jen.

Sam pulled Becky aside and showed her the black wedding cake design.

"Wow—cool." Becky's response surprised Sam.

"Glad you like it because you'll be up to your elbows in black decorations for most of the week," Sam said.

"Well, it's going to be different. But I like that." The head decorator studied the sketch intently. "I assume we'll do the ruffles from fondant and the lace out of modeling chocolate?"

"Right. Black-tinted modeling chocolate, too, for the witch hat, the wand, and the potion bottles."

"How about if we personalized the potion bottles somehow ... maybe a his and hers? I'm assuming that even though the bride thinks she's a witch, and who knows *what* the groom thinks, there's still got to be a romantic element here, right? We've got to keep it from being all about darkness and sorcery."

"Yes—that makes me feel a lot better," Sam said. "I was having a hard time yesterday wrapping my head around the concept of it. I mean, I'm all for magic and marriage kind of meaning the same thing, you know. But romance and lightheartedness need to be there too."

Becky's eyes narrowed in concentration. "I've got some ideas already. Leave it to me."

"Thank you." Sam felt one of the week's burdens lift.

"Okay," she said, "I might as well mention it while we're

talking about black decorations—the cake for the party at Ivan's. I woke up thinking we could go with some of the same ideas. The Chocoholics, of course, want chocolate—their cake can't be tinted vanilla sponge. So we'll do a deep devil's food for them. We can go with some eighty-percent cacao for the frosting so it's darker than usual, then use little lacy bits and witchy things. What do you think?"

Becky gave a little grin. "Why not? I'll make extra of any little items that look good enough for both cakes."

"Run with it. I'm going to concentrate on the birthday cakes. We have one due this afternoon, two on Friday and one Saturday," Sam said, spreading order forms across the end of the table and prioritizing them by delivery date.

She had no sooner pulled the layers for the first one out of the walk-in fridge than she heard a familiar voice out front. A minute later Rupert came floating through the split in the curtain that separated the sales room from the kitchen. Sam laughed at herself for thinking of his movements that way, but it was true that her old friend had a flair for the dramatic. With his usual loose pants, flowing tunic and scarf wafting over his left shoulder—not to mention his six-foot portly frame—Rupert wasn't the sort who blended into the background.

"Ah, Samantha, my dear," he gushed, planting a kiss on her cheek. "Lovely, as always."

"Rupe, you're a case." She knew she had a smear of orange frosting across the breast of her white baker's jacket and most likely there were dabs of black somewhere on her face. "Or, you are mocking me."

"I never mock. You know that."

It was true. Rupert was one of the kindest men on earth—to his friends. In print, it was another story. He wrote bestselling steamy romance novels under the pen name Victoria DeVane and was known for placing his characters in situations where they made rampant fun of politics and religion and society in general. Sam was one of the very few, aside from his editor in New York, who knew Victoria's true identity.

"You know about the party at the bookstore on Saturday?" he asked.

Sam nodded. "And I heard about your play. Zoë says she's starring. So, what's it about?" She scooped buttercream frosting into a pastry bag as they talked.

"Uh-uh—can't tell you that," he said, wagging a finger. "I will only say there's going to be an unexpected surprise ending. I've just been next door, working with Ivan to set up the venue."

Only Rupert used words like *venue* when talking about a neighborhood bookstore.

"We shall move some things around and create a little stage and there will be plenty of chairs for the audience. I have even convinced him to rig up some stage lighting."

"Really?" Sam couldn't imagine how all this would fit into the quaint bookshop.

"Mostly, it involves rearranging the furniture in the reading area and re-aiming track lighting to point to one end of the room," he admitted. "But, I refuse to think small-scale. It will be glorious in its own way."

Sam raised an eyebrow. Glorious?

"Now if we can keep those new bookstore cats from being underfoot."

"Cats? I don't remember Ivan having cats."

"A rather new addition, I'm afraid. Ivan hired a new girl last month. Now, it seems Edgar and Agatha have come along with her."

"I met Alex awhile back but didn't know about her cats. That sounds like fun. People love animals in shops. I mean, I haven't had a kitten since I was a kid, and we certainly can't have pets here because of the health codes, but I've heard they're very popular in bookstores. Their names certainly go along with the mystery theme, don't they?"

Rupert grumbled a small acknowledgement. Sam recalled one of his previous partners bringing a cat into the home they shared. Mark's cat had become a character—both in the figurative sense and when it landed a role in one of Rupert's books. She wondered if his attitude had changed or it was more a matter that Alex's cats might upstage his Halloween production.

"Well, must go," he said. "I'm taking a delightful man to lunch. Pop over to Ivan's if you have a chance and see what you think of the furniture arrangement." With that, he breezed to the front of the shop and she heard the bells jingle his departure.

Sam started to work on the simple layer cake for today's birthday party, a golden slipper design. As she smoothed pink buttercream around the sides of it she thought about Rupert's invitation. With the stack of orders currently sitting on her desk, it didn't seem there would be any popping-over anytime soon.

Chapter 4

Sam had just set the golden slipper on top of the birthday cake for her customer's little princess when the back door opened.

"Hi, Mom!" Kelly's aquamarine eyes sparkled and her brown curls bounced.

Sam wondered what good news had created the buoyant mood, something good enough for her daughter to take a break in the middle of the morning. Maybe there'd been a lull in the number of unkempt dogs arriving at Puppy Chic, the grooming salon next door to the east. Normally the owner, Riki Davis-Jones did the heavy clipping, while Kelly's duties mainly involved baths for the canine clients.

"We heard about the party," Kelly said, her dimples showing. "Riki's going, and Ivan said I could bring Scott. Do you think he and I would make a great Indiana Jones and Marion? I don't know … are they considered literary? I first thought Harry Potter and Ginny Weasley … but I'm thinking it might be tough to convince Scott to be a teenage wizard. So, what do you think?"

"I think you better remember to breathe," Sam said with a laugh.

Becky piped up. "I can easily see Scott as Indy. He is a history professor, after all. He probably already has a bullwhip."

Kelly blushed, Becky blushed, and Sam didn't dare ask what that was about. Her daughter had only started dating this new man a few weeks ago.

"What about you, Julio? What costume are you wearing?" Becky paused in the middle of piping a huge chocolate rose.

Julio only grunted.

"You are going to the party, aren't you? We're all invited. You'll get to see everyone enjoying the cake we're baking for them."

Sam realized she knew practically nothing about Julio's personal life. He might have a wife and six kids at home, as far as she knew. He seemed content with his work but he rarely joined in the workplace camaraderie. Which was okay. His baking skills were what she paid for and a person was allowed a private life. She flashed Becky a look that said *leave it alone*.

"What's your costume, Becky?" Kelly asked, wiping a dab of chocolate frosting off the worktable and licking it from her finger.

"I don't know. If I come, it'll probably be a quick drop-by. My kids will be nagging us to go trick-or-treating and either Don or I need to be home to hand out treats. Last year I dressed as a princess and answered the door in costume. I could dig that one up again, I suppose."

"Sure—you could put on your costume here, drop by the bookstore for a little while, and you can still get home in time to be with your kids," Kelly suggested. "What about you, Mom? Do you have your costume?"

All eyes turned to Sam. "Well, it won't be a couple's theme. Beau's job pretty much guarantees he won't be able to go. I doubt he'll even see me in my costume. But, no, I haven't thought of anything yet."

Kelly went back to her job and Sam put the princess cake into the fridge so the icing would set before the customer arrived in the afternoon to pick it up. While she kneaded black color paste into a big ball of fondant, the others drifted back to their regular work.

"I found this lace pattern we could use to romanticize the black wedding cake a bit," Becky said. She spread the drawing on the table.

"Good. What about the other touches?"

"Remember how I suggested we personalize the potion bottles … make them his and hers? How about I'll make one hot pink and one electric blue and write something on each?"

A picture flashed into Sam's head. "The spell book that forms the basis for the cake … We could write something there in white or silver script. 'Mix potions in equal parts to brew up a forever love.' It's not quite poetic enough, but something like that."

"I like it," said Becky. She began jotting notes on the order form.

The days passed in a blur of activity; by Friday, Sam had to admit the black wedding cake had become impressive under Becky's capable touch. The open book with its stream of silver sparkles, the potion bottles and wand set the theme on the bottom tier. Together Sam and Becky had made yards of fondant ruffles and carefully placed them around the middle tier, the romantic layer as Becky called it. Black lace, silver buttons and black poppies added elegance. A perky witch's hat capped the top tier, set at a jaunty angle with roses around the band as Becky imagined a real witch might wear for her wedding.

The color had proven to be the tricky part but Jen's suggestion of creating faint variations in shading made all the difference. Every rose and each petal stood out in its own special way. Sam gave the whole cake a light spritz of very fine transparent glitter. When she stepped back, the sight almost took her breath away.

Becky actually let out a tiny squeal.

Jen came through the curtain and stopped in her tracks. "It's amazing."

"I have to admit I didn't have great hopes for this concept when the customer ordered it," Sam said. "But she was right. Just goes to show—I'm not always the one with the great ideas."

Jen said, "Maybe. But you two had the skill to pull it off. I'll call Cass right away. She is going to love her cake!"

"Tell her I can deliver it as soon as I'm finished here," Sam said, sending the last of the icing-crusted decorator tools into the sink full of hot, sudsy water.

She sank onto the chair at her desk. It had been a long week. Saturday morning would bring customers picking up their party foods—cupcakes and cookies in the tens of dozens, a few specialty cakes, and delivery of another wedding cake. Sam would put the final touches on the cake for Ivan's party, although she'd been working on it alongside the one for Cassie Wolinsky since many of the elements were similar.

The only thing she still had not addressed was her costume for the party.

Julio finished washing up and said goodnight. Becky had left shortly after snapping photos of their first all-black cake for the bakery's album and helping Sam load it into her van. Sam could hear Jen out front saying goodbye to a customer. Soon she would close and tally the register receipts and leave.

Sam picked up her bag and keys, reminded Jen to lock up, and re-checked the Wolinsky address as the van warmed up. Past the plaza she cruised, not needing to check street names—the house was only a couple of blocks from where Sam had lived before she married Beau. She spotted the black and silver Mini Cooper in a driveway and stopped her van at the curb.

"Oh, yay!" Cassie shrieked, barreling out the front door. She rushed to join Sam at the back of the van. "Ohmygod, it's beautiful! *So* perfect!"

Sam smiled with relief. She had managed to please another picky bride. "The two of us can carry it. Do you have a table set up for it inside?"

"For tonight, it's going in the dining room. The ceremony will actually take place out in the forest tomorrow. We have everything set up—there'll be a bonfire, fairy garlands, and then the full moon—"

"Sounds pretty amazing."

"It will be. Everyone's really excited about it."

Cass warned Sam about a step up to the front porch. They situated the cake amidst a clutter of party plates, stacks of plastic cups, a dayglow green punch bowl and boxes of decorations. After cautioning Cass to be sure the cake remained in a cool place and stayed upright, Sam left. Oh, to be so young and enthused, she mused as she turned her thoughts back to her own duties for Halloween.

At the first traffic light, Sam closed her eyes and tried to envision what she might wear to Ivan's party. She'd already ruled out a glamour costume—no Phryne Fisher with her roaring '20s slender gowns, no Irene Adler—and she couldn't quite see herself in jeans and boots as Kinsey Millhone, carrying a gun and kicking ass. Nothing in her closet had suggested anything; she'd checked it three times already. Maybe a visit to the thrift shop would spark an idea.

Chapter 5

Saturday night. Sam couldn't believe how the week had slipped by. The final customer walked out the door at six. Sweet's Sweets was closed for the weekend now and Sam planned to relax and simply have some fun. Becky in her lovely princess gown had carried the Chocoholics cake next door, where the party was already underway. Parking spots in front of the short row of shops were at a premium and she noticed most of the metered spaces along the street were also taken.

Jen wanted her costume to be a surprise, saying she would go home to change and come along soon. Sam hadn't wanted to take the time to drive all the way out to the ranch, change clothes and come back so she had simply brought everything in a garment bag. She turned out the shop's lights except for the one nighttime lamp.

In the bathroom she rinsed off the dusting of sugar which always coated her face and arms by end of day, then she pulled out the old-fashioned 1940s dress. Simple and plain, with a vintage hat and sturdy shoes, she hoped she would be the only one in the guise of Miss Marple.

The dress seemed a little tighter than when she'd tried it on yesterday, darn it. It zipped up when she held her stomach in. Women of the era certainly had been slimmer. Well, she reasoned, it would provide the best excuse not to eat much. With the shoes and hat in place, a light touch of lipstick and blush, she felt she carried off the role quite well. Agatha Christie would be proud of her.

The bookshop had, indeed, been transformed just as Rupert predicted. Strands of fairy lights circled the windows and crisscrossed the room. Sam could see people milling about inside, most having arrived an hour or more earlier. She watched the scene for a moment before walking in. Tinkling music, faintly haunting and more than a little spooky, filled the room. At least Ivan avoided hard rock or recordings of anguished screams—thank heaven for small favors. She spotted their host dressed as Sherlock Holmes, albeit a rather short version, standing near his desk and surveying the room.

Sam saw a Count Dracula talking to Riki, who was cute as could be as The Cat in the Hat.

A large table normally filled with bargain books now held food to fit the Halloween theme—meatballs dripping blood-red sauce, ribs appropriately charred, and cheese canapes with something that made them look eerily like eyeballs were among the offerings. Grave-marker cookies, ghostly white cupcakes and the fabulous (if she did say so herself) black-on-black witchy cake filled the dessert table to perfection. Becky had even thought to bring a small stack of Sam's business cards to let everyone know where the goodies had originated.

Princess Becky caught Sam's eye and walked up to her. "I love your dress," she said. "Who are you?"

Oh dear. Sam could picture herself explaining her costume to everyone she met. She would have to adopt an English accent, if a girl originally from Texas could possibly manage such a feat.

"I need to skip out," Becky said once she had thoroughly approved Miss Marple. "I think the pastries are all squared away, but if Ivan needs anything more Jen should be here any minute to help out."

Kelly and Scott had, indeed, come as Indiana Jones and Marion. Kelly had her camera phone aimed at an elegantly dressed couple; the blond woman in the blue Victorian dress was one Sam vaguely remembered from the Chocoholics group. In addition to a couple more Sherlocks, she saw a Gatsby/Daisy pair, a sexy black cat and a troll; it seemed adherence to the mystery theme had relaxed a bit.

She spotted Rupert across the room, attired in his usual flowing style, this time all-brown with a dramatic sixteenth-century hat with a long feather that swept down to his shoulder. He seemed somewhat agitated, his gaze darting in a dozen directions. Sam made her way through the crowd toward him.

"Miss Marple," he said, "lovely to see you."

"Thank you, my dear." She didn't even come close to pulling off the accent and reverted to her normal voice. "Sorry. At least you recognized my character."

"But you have not quite puzzled out mine, have you?" He gave a subtle wink. "I am the playwright tonight, love, and also leading man in the play, a woodsman."

"Shakespeare?" She didn't recall having ever seen a picture of the famed poet in such a flourishing hat, but leeway could always be granted on Halloween, she supposed.

Sam's interest was piqued but he refused to say more about his story line. Again, he seemed restless. She rubbed a place on her neck where the lace collar of her dress itched and looked around, recognizing only a few people since nearly everyone was masked. It was an aspect she'd not considered for her own costume. "Where's Zoë?"

"Ah, tragedy there. She's been stricken with a stomach flu and is unable to grace our presence." He waved an arm dramatically.

A little less flamboyant speech would be all right, Sam thought, even though coming from him it worked.

"So, the play? What will you do?"

For once, Rupert didn't have a ready answer. He clutched a ratty-looking old book and some other sheets of paper against his chest. Then a witch stepped up to them.

When she lifted her mask—complete with green face, hooked nose and warts—Sam saw it was the lovely Darlene Trawl, one of the Chocoholics Unanimous book group members. Funny, Sam would have pictured her more as V.I. Warshawski—30-something, hip and modern. Maybe it was her long, dark curls that gave her the idea to come as a witch. Or, she already owned the requisite striped socks.

"I heard what you said just now," Darlene admitted. "I can help."

Rupert looked slightly down his nose. "I remember you. Earlier, you expressed an interest in buying the book I brought as a prop."

"I'm still interested, but we can talk about that later. About the play—I have stage experience," said Darlene, with a flash of even teeth and dimples. "I was head of my Little Theater group in Kansas before I moved here. I'm a quick study for the lines. Let me see your script."

Rupert actually seemed at a loss for words as he handed over a few pages stapled at one edge. The three of them had moved partially behind one of the tall bookshelves that formed a makeshift backstage area. An identically sized shelf ten feet away left an open area where Sam noticed for the first time a foot-high platform had been brought in to serve as a stage. Above, track lighting was aimed toward the stage, upon which sat a large black cauldron. A few potted plants were meant to give the idea the setting was in a forest.

"Okay, got it," Darlene said.

The play apparently consisted of one or two scenes with the two actors, and Sam guessed at perhaps a dramatic finish as something would foam up or emit smoke from the cauldron.

"Really," Rupert said. "You think you have the whole part memorized?"

"Let's do a quick rehearsal," Darlene suggested, handing the script back to him.

The two of them stepped a little farther out of sight of the rest of the room and Darlene said her first line, giving the words a witchy cackle. Sam heard Rupert reply as she walked back to join Ivan and the other guests. Jen had arrived, spangled to the max as Cleopatra, and three young males had gathered around.

"Miss Samantha! Or to say, good evening, Miss Marple," said Ivan. "Offering you something to drink? A lovely blood-red wine is here and some other ones. In the bowl of green punch is something brought by my assistant Alex. She tell me the smoke it is coming from … how do you say? … dry ice? Is too weird for my liking."

Alex, dressed as a student of Hogwarts, stepped up to say hello. "It's fruit punch that began with lemonade and some green food coloring. Taste carefully, though. I saw an ogre tipping the vodka bottle over it. At least he first asked me whether there would be children at the party and I told him no."

Sam started to thank her when she sensed activity at the back of the room. Rupert stood ready to make an announcement and Ivan momentarily dimmed the lights.

"Seats, everyone! Take your seats. The evening's entertainment, my original play entitled *Curse of the Forest,* will begin shortly. Please be seated."

Guests headed toward the three rows of folding chairs set up facing the small stage. Sam accepted a glass of the red wine and stood near the door. With the first sip she realized what a long day it had been, and the lace collar was seriously beginning to bug her. Well, she would stay for Rupert's play, be certain she'd greeted her own customers and make her excuses for an early exit.

Ivan fiddled with light switches near his sales counter, bringing up small spotlights aimed at the stage. Once their audience was nearly settled, he and Rupert exchanged a nod and the room went dark.

Rupert cleared his throat lightly and the stage lights gradually came up as Ivan operated the dimmer control. Sam was vaguely aware of Ivan slipping over to the food table as Rupert took the stage.

He swished his cape and looked back over his shoulder, as if speaking to an unseen companion.

"Careful, lad, the forest is rumored to be the haven of

witches and 'tis the one night of the year when one doesn't
want to cross a witch's path." He noticed the cauldron
and stopped short, motioning to his invisible friend not to
approach.

From the opposite side of the stage, the green-faced
witch emerged with her right-hand fingers spread like
claws, the tatty old book clutched in her left hand, her
demeanor sneaky and threatening. Sam had to admit, for
short-notice acting, Darlene was doing a pretty good job.
She thought of Zoë, missing out on her acting debut, and
made herself a mental note to call later and find out how
her friend was feeling.

The witch let out a delighted cackle at the sight of the
man in her forest. Rupert overplayed his shock but the
audience loved it.

"Come here, my man," said the witch, crooking her
finger toward him.

Rupert shook his head and dashed away. From her
angle, Sam could see him leap off the platform then turn
to be ready to enter again on cue. The witch faced the
audience, her green mask giving everyone the evil eye. She
turned toward the cauldron, opened her spell book, and
uttered an incantation of some sort.

The witch had barely said the words when the lights
went out.

The audience waited, certain the plot was about to get
even more dramatic. A couple of loud thumps came from
the stage area. Then a crash.

Rupert shouted. "What happened? Get the lights, Ivan!
Get the lights!"

Sam felt movement beside her and heard Ivan muttering
something in Russian. A long thirty seconds passed before

he got to the switches by the desk. When the lights came back on, Sam watched Rupert dash onstage and kneel. Many in the audience stood and someone in the front row screamed.

Rupert looked up, stricken, and Sam caught a glimpse of Darlene lying near the cauldron. A puddle of blood began to flow across the floor.

It appeared the wicked witch was dead.

Chapter 6

Dracula rushed forward, stating he was an EMT, and tugged the rubber mask from Darlene's face. From Sam's perspective she couldn't see what he was doing but it was less than half a minute before he looked up at Rupert and shook his head.

Rupert closed his eyes, his face contorted as the nightmare came true in front of him. Sam pushed her way toward him as the rest of the crowd went chaotic. When she touched his arm, he started.

The EMT looked up.

"My husband is the sheriff," Sam told him. "I'm calling him now."

Her proper little Miss Marple handbag held her cell phone and she called Beau's personal phone.

"Hey, darlin'. Sorry I'm missing the party but things are a little nuts here at the moment."

Sam stepped behind the tall bookcase for a little more privacy.

"There's a problem and I'm calling officially," she said. "A woman has been killed here at the bookstore. I have no idea how, but it looks like a murder. We need you right away."

He sucked in his breath. "Well, there's a little problem with that. I'm on a routine traffic stop and some naked guy just dashed out of an alley and stole my cruiser."

"What?" Sam couldn't wrap her mind around the scenario.

He repeated what he'd just said. "It's probably some stupid Halloween prank but I have to track it down before the guy wrecks a valuable piece of county equipment. Let me contact dispatch. I'll send a deputy to your location. Don't let anyone leave and don't let them near the body. I'll be along as soon as I can."

Sam felt her insides quaver as he ended the call. Just when she really needed his steady presence. She took a deep breath and dug for some sort of deep inner strength. People were milling about divided, it seemed, between the squeamish, the hysterical and the morbidly curious.

Rupert stared at the stage area, stunned, and Sam went to his side. The young EMT came closest to being in charge—at least he'd kept anyone else from setting foot on the raised platform. Possibly, no one wanted to mess with Dracula.

Sam told both men what Beau had said. "We need to keep everyone here."

Rupert gathered himself, taking a deep breath, letting his theatrical training put him into the role of a calm man in charge. He caught Ivan's eye and the music, which had become irritating by now, quit.

"Ladies and gentlemen," Rupert announced in a voice that carried to the farthest corners. "I'm afraid there's been a tragedy and we all must keep our wits about us. The authorities are on their way. Everyone must stay inside the store until the sheriff arrives to sort it out. You'll be asked what you saw and it's important you cooperate with them."

Sam sent him a tiny smile of encouragement.

"Meanwhile, remain calm and ..." He paused. "Have some cake?"

It was rare to see Rupert at a loss for words. Sam touched his hand as he turned away from the crowd.

"You okay?" she asked.

"The poor woman. One must empathize, even when it's someone we didn't actually know."

Sam nodded. Her gaze fell to the stage area near the cauldron. "Rupert, did you pick up your book?"

His head snapped around, following her stare. "No! Oh, god, it's gone!"

Before she could stop him, he had leaped onto the platform and marched over to the cauldron. The EMT, who seemed to have taken charge of watching over the area, reached out but couldn't quite grab Rupert. The nervous conversation in the room screeched to a dead halt.

Rupert seized his moment. "The book—the witch character was holding a book. Has anyone seen it?"

Sam looked over the crowd. Blank stares, confused glances among themselves. She saw Kelly and Scott hovering at the far side of the group, near the store's front door. Jen, in her elegant Cleopatra gown, was talking quietly with Riki, who still wore her big striped hat.

"I must ask again," Rupert said. "Has anyone seen the old book that was on this stage a few minutes ago?"

No one responded and, despite the EMT's efforts to herd Rupert from the stage, the big man walked behind the cauldron and to each end of the platform but found no sign of his book. How on earth could someone have killed Darlene, snatched the book, and gotten away so quickly? Sam wondered. The lights had been off for a minute at most.

To her relief, red and blue strobes flashed at the front windows as a cruiser pulled into the parking lot and stopped behind several of the parked cars. She recognized Rico, one of Beau's deputies. He spoke into his shoulder mike, gave a little tug at his accessory-laden belt and strode toward the door. All attention went that direction and a pathway through the crowd automatically opened as Rico entered.

He picked Ivan out of the gathering, spotting the owner behind the sales desk. "This is your shop?"

Ivan nodded.

"Sorry for the damper on your party, but we need to keep everyone inside."

Ivan nodded again. Sam noticed he always had a meek way around law enforcement. It had taken him more than a year to be able to say hello to Beau.

Rico spotted Sam and Rupert near the stage, where Dracula-medic stood guard over Darlene's body. Despite the heavy makeup, the deputy recognized the EMT and greeted him by name.

"Glad you were here, Phil. Tell me what happened."

The recount seemed accurate to Sam, what she heard of it, as Rico took down the basic who-what-where information. She found herself watching out for her own little brood—Kelly and Scott hovered near the back of the crowd, joined now by Jen and Riki. Most everyone talked quietly amongst themselves, disinterested in food or drink. Rupert kept pacing the back of the store, sending glances toward the shelves of books, perhaps hoping to spot his missing one.

"What was it about the book?" Sam asked him in a low tone. "I know that's what is worrying you."

He shrugged. "The volume purported to be a book of spells. Initially, its battered appearance caught my attention—something I could photograph and supply for the artwork on my newest book cover. When I purchased it I envisioned something of use in my writing research, thinking it might have definitions of things such as witch's bane or some such. I'm working on an historical novel set in Romania and thought it might provide me with some ideas. I'd no idea anyone else would know anything about it, nor would they care."

"But it seems Darlene did care."

"In the minutes before the play started I had handed it to her and she was on her side of the 'wings' hungrily paging through it as though there were something of vital interest to her."

"I wonder what?"

"I've no idea."

Chapter 7

Deputy Rico's questions were becoming a bit pointed, Sam thought, as he turned his attention toward Rupert.

"How close were you standing to the victim when the lights went out?" Rico's pencil hovered over his notepad.

"At that moment I was stage left, awaiting my cue, which was the line 'A sound?' The witch had heard a sound from the forest and I was to appear, just in time to be overtaken by the spell she had said over the cauldron."

"Let's talk in terms of Darlene Trawl and Rupert Penrick, rather than the acting parts you were playing."

"The facts remain. Darlene was to recite a given line, and I was to step onto the stage. But everything went dark before my foot actually touched the boards."

"Sam, you said you were at the front of the store, near

the cashier desk, and Ivan operated the light switches from there, right?"

"Yes, but Ivan moved to the food table as soon as the play started."

"So, since he wasn't within reach of the switches at that moment, how did the lights go out?"

"I'm not sure. In my shop there are electrical switches near the back door to the alley. This store must have the same, but I don't think anyone was back there. It's Ivan's stock room where he keeps extra books and cleaning supplies. You'd have to ask him."

Rupert was on his way to the stock room the moment she said it, and Rico took off to chase him down. The lights flicked off and someone shrieked, but the room lit up again immediately.

"—probably destroyed fingerprints," Rico was saying as he led Rupert back by the cuff of his voluminous jacket.

Rupert looked somewhat chastised but there was a glint of satisfaction too. "The back door was standing ajar," he said to Sam. "It has to be how the killer came and went and how he controlled the lights."

Rico fixed him with a stern stare. "Do not touch another thing, and do not go wandering around." He seemed a little overwhelmed at having to control this many people and this large a crime scene on his own.

Sam took him aside. "Beau has deputized me on other cases. I can help if you like."

He gave her Miss Marple outfit the once-over and clearly wasn't wild about her suggestion, but he didn't have a lot of options until more official help arrived.

"We'll need to search the alley and the back room for evidence. For now, though, the best we can do is secure the area to be sure no vehicle drives through and no person has access. Can you come up with a way to do that?"

"Sure." Somehow.

She recruited Scott and Kelly and they rounded up a variety of trash barrels and cardboard cartons from Puppy Chic and the bakery, plus a couple of barricades from a power-company project nearby, and used their finds to form rather creative stacks at each end of the alley. When Beau arrived they could add official yellow tape but for now this would suffice.

Halfway through the job, Sam's costume was binding her armpits, constricting her chest and the lace collar had rubbed a raw spot on her neck. By the end, she was ready to strip it off right there in public.

"I'm changing clothes," she told Kelly as she unlocked the door to her shop. "If Rico asks, I'll be back in a couple minutes."

Relief was immediate once Sam had her normal black pants and white baker's jacket on. Screw the costumes—Halloween had lost its magic for her this year. She took her first deep breath of the evening and walked back to the bookstore.

Her hand was on the doorknob when a vehicle arrived behind her. Beau. Thank goodness.

She waited as he emerged from a squad car, not his normal department SUV.

"Naked guy still got your car?" she teased.

"Thankfully, no. Two of our men stopped him about six blocks from where he took it. But, ugh, don't even get me started. The man was drunk as a skunk and, well, let's just say there are cleanup issues before I'm getting in that vehicle again. In fact, this might be my year to request a new one."

"Eww—I'm not even going there. Picture me with my

fingers in my ears saying la-la-la-la."

He tilted his head toward the bookshop. "So, what happened here? A murder at a party? Are you okay, Sam?"

She swallowed the emotion that hit when he expressed concern. "I'm doing okay. Rico kept me busy. As far as the crime itself, it all happened so fast."

She told him about the play and the witch and the book, how the lights went out and about the thumping sounds in the dark, the pool of blood around the body. "I don't even know yet what killed her. I didn't see any sort of weapon nearby—not that I wanted to get very close."

"I'll call in the crime scene tech. Most of tonight's action around town hasn't been quite this violent, and I think she's free." He placed the call. Before they went into the shop, Sam filled him in on the open back door and how they had blocked the alley.

"Let's see what we got," he said, setting a gentle hand on her back as they walked into the bookstore together.

Shock had clearly set in with some of the guests, while others were pacing impatiently and griping that they wanted to leave. They had other, more fun places to be. A cloth had been draped over the body and the guests studiously avoided the stage area and back of the room. They'd also abandoned the food. Not so much the liquor—the level in the punch bowl was down quite a bit.

Beau quickly divided the guests into groups based on a few astute questions. Members of the Chocoholics group, those who knew Darlene Trawl best, were asked to remain; those who had been nearest the stage were also held back for a few more questions. People who had never met the victim got away with only having to leave their names and contact information. Immediately, it thinned the crowd by more than half.

Sam felt the shift in focus. No longer was it a milling crowd of impatient ghouls and ghosts. Those who remained had more specific reasons to be concerned—they could be considered suspects.

Chapter 8

The same set of questions, asked more than a dozen times—Sam was impressed with how well Beau handled it, staying alert and yet distancing himself from the tiny dramas which played out with nearly everyone there. After the initial weeding-out of guests, she left Beau and Rico to handle the interrogations.

Lisa, the crime scene investigator for the department, was nearly finished doing her bit. An autopsy would be needed, naturally, but she immediately pointed out a stab wound so close to the victim's heart it almost certainly had to be the cause of death. Once Darlene Trawl's body had been taken away by the medical investigator's office, Lisa finished examining the stage area and moved on to the alley behind the building.

Beau's questions, knowing a sharp weapon was involved,

turned to costumes and accessories. Which characters carried a knife or sword? Were they all accounted for now? Had anyone seen such a weapon either before or after the stabbing? While the men asked their questions, she prowled around the shop, wondering if the book might have been quickly stashed on a shelf somewhere.

"I haven't found it either," said Rupert, coming up beside her. "Somebody wanted that book awfully badly, didn't they?"

"One thing I've learned from Beau is not to guess at motives until a lot more facts are known."

She pictured the moment before the room went into darkness, with Darlene the witch holding the book. Then it hit her—originally, Zoë was to play the part of the witch. Her best friend could have been the victim if all had gone according to plan. Her hands suddenly began to shake.

"Sam? You okay?"

She nodded absently and Rupert moved on.

Why take a chance on murdering someone so publicly, she reasoned once she forced herself to think logically. If the killer only wanted the book, he or she would have used the darkness as cover and snatched it or simply found a time when it was easy to break into Rupert's home and take it.

There was something more to this whole puzzle and Sam couldn't quite wrap her mind around it. The fact that it was almost ten p.m. and she'd been on the go since five this morning didn't help. But to go home now … she knew she wouldn't sleep as long as Beau and many of her friends were here. She needed to be doing something. Standing around and watching Beau do his work, made her feel like a useless fixture in the room.

She thought again of her theory about Zoë. To be on

the safe side, she pulled out her phone and called her best friend's home number. Darryl answered and said Zoë was feeling better but had gone to bed early. Sam recapped the bookstore events with as little drama as possible, while making the point that they didn't yet know for certain if Darlene Trawl had been the intended victim. Someone could have assumed Zoë was the person inside the witch's mask.

"What are you saying, Sam? Do we need to be watching for some unseen enemy?"

"I don't know, Darryl." Sam couldn't think of anyone on earth less likely to have an enemy. Her concern felt almost ridiculous. "Just be aware, I guess. If any of your guests are acting weird or a stranger comes around ..." It sounded lame.

He thanked her for her concern and asked Sam to keep them posted on the investigation. Hopefully the killer would be found quickly, he said.

Most likely, Rupert's idea that the crime was somehow centered around the book was correct.

Sam saw Beau across the room where he had gathered the book club members. Being the group who knew the victim best, they might shed light on something from Darlene's personal life. Sam decided to listen in. She borrowed a small notepad from Ivan's desk to jot down impressions, not trusting her memory with details this late in the evening.

"Eight of us," said a blond woman in a blue Victorian dress with a purple ostrich feather on her hat. "I suppose I'm the unofficial leader. We take turns choosing the book we'll read each time but if no one has picked one, I do it. I also take responsibility for scheduling the meetings and contacting everyone if there's a change of plans."

"So, Mrs. Pritchard, you can tell me if anyone from the club is missing tonight," Beau said.

Sam recognized Amy Pritchard as an occasional bakery customer.

Amy looked around the six people gathered nearby. "Lila Bayles couldn't make it—a head cold, I think. She's in her eighties, so the idea of her sneaking back here and attacking Darlene is ridiculous."

A couple of the others, including Riki, snickered at the suggestion.

"Harry Taylor isn't here. I don't know why. He normally comes to every meeting unless the chosen book contains too much romance. He's mostly fond of thrillers with plenty of action and a bit of gore, not that we choose those often."

"But Harry is another iffy choice," Riki said. "The man has to be seventy and he walks with such a limp I hardly see him sprinting out the back door."

A younger member, male, with longish brown hair dressed as Sherlock Holmes spoke up. "Riki's right. Harry might have personality issues—he's a total curmudgeon—but I don't see him in a physical attack." He sent a moon-eyed smile Riki's direction.

"You're Pete Winters, right?" Beau asked. "I've asked everyone else, but didn't get the chance to talk to you yet—did your costume include any type of sharp object, such as a knife?"

"As Sherlock Holmes? No! The worst he would carry would be an opium pipe—but there's no way I have that either." Flustered, he began to over-explain.

Beau seemed to be studying the voluminous overcoat

Pete wore, wondering what the pockets might contain. But surely the man could not be so dumb as to flee out the back door and then come back without dumping the bloody knife first—Sam read Beau's thoughts as well as if he'd spoken them aloud.

When Pete's protests subsided Beau turned to the man standing behind Amy Pritchard.

"I'm Alan Pritchard," he said. "The man behind the boss here."

He patted Amy's shoulder and she drew back slightly. Alan made a very polished Max DeWinter with his dark good looks and perfectly tailored tuxedo of the era.

"I attend book club meetings occasionally but I'm not really a regular. The book has to grab my interest."

"He misses the whole spirit of the Chocoholics Unanimous, which is an avid love of chocolate," Amy said, not bothering to look up at her husband.

Sam, who had been writing all the names on her notepad, noted the dismissive attitude between them.

"What about Keith? Where is he right now?" Pete Winters asked.

"Mr. Trawl was taken home before his wife's body was removed," Beau said. "I've sent another deputy to be with him. Was Keith also a member of the book group?"

"At times," Amy responded. "I invited him personally in the beginning."

Some ripple passed through the group. Sam couldn't quite decipher it, but realized she might chalk that up to her own weariness.

No one seemed to have much to add, and after a couple of clarification questions Beau told them they could go home. Sam caught Ivan's eye. The poor bookseller looked exhausted. What a bad turn his party evening had taken.

Chapter 9

Sam opened her eyes Sunday morning to full daylight in their upstairs bedroom, delighted at the unusual sleep-in. Then the memory of their later-than-normal evening and the reason dampened her good mood.

"Wow, nine o'clock," Beau said, rolling over and taking her in his arms.

"I don't know how you do it," she said. "Dealing with murder, the victim, her family, the suspects. And then you wake up cheerful and ready to do it again."

He set a gentle kiss on her temple. "Well, first off, we don't have a whole lot of murders in Taos County. Luckily. If I worked homicide in a big city, I'd burn out real fast. Last night was your first time as an eyewitness. That had to be hard. I wish I could rewind and let you have a carefree evening at a fun party."

"Me too," she said, rising up to one elbow and looking into his ocean-blue eyes.

"At least you have the day at home to do whatever you want. I still need to go to the office. I can't let an extra day go by before I start seriously working this case. It worries me—already there are so many flaws that will make it a heyday for a defense attorney, *if* we can nail down a suspect and make the case strong enough for the prosecutor to tackle it."

"Flaws, like what?"

He got out of bed and pulled on his jeans. "Let me count the ways … the body was touched, someone draped a cloth over it, the stage area had been walked on, any number of vehicles could have driven through the alley before the barriers went up. I'm not saying you guys didn't do all the right things. You did. There were just too many people around."

"You're right, but doesn't that happen a lot?"

"More than we'd like," he said, fastening the pearl snaps on his western shirt. "Few crime scenes are pristine enough that only the victim and his or her killer were there. Still, we do catch most of the bad guys."

Sam sat up and leaned against the headboard.

"Stay in bed awhile," he said. "I'm going to check on the horses and then I'm making breakfast for you. Waffles or French toast?"

"I love your French toast. I'll come down in a minute and help," she said, leaving the warmth of the comforter and heading for the shower.

When Beau came into the kitchen fifteen minutes later, he smelled of oats, fresh air and frost. At the table, conversation kept coming back to the previous night's events.

"Do you think Darlene was the real target, Beau?" Sam asked, accepting the pitcher of warm syrup he handed over. "I had the worst feeling it could have been Zoë up on that stage. Supposing Rupert's book was the real reason for the crime, I would have lost my best friend last night. I called their house while you were questioning people. I had to be sure she was okay."

He sent her a reassuring smile. "I can't imagine any way Zoë was the intended target. True, we're lucky she wasn't the one in the witch costume. Beyond that, we just don't know yet."

Sam knew he was right. She also knew he would say nearly anything to ease her worries.

"I can't help but believe the killer was someone in the store, a costumed partygoer. Otherwise, how would he know the precise moment to come in through the back door and rush the stage?"

"Someone knew about the set of light switches near the back door, too. Knew they could turn off the lights and get to the stage in moments. I'll tell you this, honey, if you promise not to hold it against my deputy. Rico initially suspected Rupert might have snatched the book and planned to hide it and file an insurance claim. Rupert *was* the closest to the victim."

"Beau! That's ridiculous. We don't even know if the old book was worth anything. He got it at a flea market for a few dollars. And secondly, Rupert has more money than he knows what to do with." She hesitated, not wanting to reveal the man's secret identity as a bestselling author. "Just trust me, he wouldn't need the money from an insurance claim on a crappy old book."

"If you say so."

"I'll go by and talk to Rupe if you'd like. I can find out what he really knew about the book, whether it was worth anything at all. And tell Rico I'm not mad at him. Like his gorgeous boss, your deputy has a job to do and I understand how he has to suspect everyone at first. But tell him he's got it all wrong about Rupert."

Sam cleared the breakfast dishes while Beau changed into his uniform. He was still driving the spare squad car, which was another probable reason for his wanting to get to work right away. With luck, maybe his own department vehicle would be sanitized and ready to reclaim.

As she had no other plans for her day off, Sam dialed Rupert's number. By the sound of his greeting, she caught him in mid-yawn.

"Rough night, wasn't it?" she said. "How are you doing this morning?"

"I've been better. I'm sure one day I'll view all this as material for a story, but right now I cannot shake the image of Darlene Trawl lying there in front of me on the floor."

"You up for some company? I've got scones from my shop leftover from yesterday. They'll make a nice breakfast."

"Scones, a pot of tea and you as a morning visitor. I can't think of anything nicer."

Sam tied a bow around the purple bakery box she'd brought home. Rupert was the sort who appreciated the little touches. Someone had given her a gold foil-wrapped packet of Marks & Spencer English tea and she added it to the gift. Thirty minutes later she was pulling up in front of Rupert's home.

"Is that Luxury Gold No. 2?" he exclaimed when he saw the tea. "Samantha, I love you. If Beau Cardwell hadn't married you first, I would have!"

She laughed aloud. "No you wouldn't. You knew me for years before I ever met Beau. Plus, all your handsome male admirers would die of jealousy."

"Too true," he said, leading the way to his gourmet kitchen. "We couldn't have that. But as a wonderful girlfriend, Sam, you're tops."

The effusive praise made her feel badly about the quizzing she was about to dish out. She watched as Rupert spooned tea into a delicate china pot and poured boiling water from the electric kettle. Gratefully, she took the cup he poured.

"I have to say, I felt completely wrung out last night," she said. "I'd never met Darlene Trawl but what happened was so unreal."

"I'd only met her once, so briefly I didn't actually remember her when she came up and offered to take Zoë's role in the play last night."

"She seemed very interested in the book you were using as a prop. I wonder why."

"She had seen it—a few days before the party. I stopped by the bookshop to have Ivan take a look. I'm sure I could have found people with more expertise, but I was curious about the old thing, whether it had any value at all. At a glance, I knew there was some sort of interesting history to the volume."

He took a scone from the box and spread lemon curd on a bite. Sam settled back in her chair and waited for the story to emerge.

"The copyright date inside the book was 1845 and the title was *Spells and Incantations For the Proficient Witch.*"

"Seriously?"

"That's what it said. Intriguing, definitely. Do I believe in that stuff? Let's say I lean toward the very skeptical."

"Don't tell me you planned to try out the spells and incantations."

"The one I marked for the witch to read in the play seemed very harmless. It was supposed to summon a good luck charm."

"Well, that didn't work out so well, did it?" Sam tentatively sipped the tea, discovered it had settled to the right temperature, and took a longer sip.

"Sadly, no. Anyway, although I thought the book made an excellent prop for the play, mainly I hoped it could provide a few fun tidbits to insert into my stories."

"Someone suggested it might be of value, which could be the reason it was taken."

"Ah yes, well, as I said, I thought I would show it to Ivan to get some idea. One would think nearly any book of that age would have some rarity, you know." He finished his first scone and reached for another. "The day I happened by there, the chocolate-loving book club had apparently just finished ripping some other poor author to shreds. They were standing around with their cupcakes—so smart of you to provide them with chocolate desserts for every meeting."

She brushed aside the compliment. Ivan actually paid for the weekly chocolates to keep the group happy and buying their books from his store.

"Did any of them show a special interest in the book?" she asked.

"Several, in fact. Let's see … Darlene and her husband were there, as well as that Pritchard woman and her husband, an older pair—Lila somebody and Harry whatshisname—

and of course your dog groomer friend, Riki. Maybe some others. Any of them could have overheard what Ivan told me about the book after he looked it up at some online site, that he felt it might be quite valuable if its condition were better. This unfortunate copy showed plenty of wear but a nicer copy could be worth well into the tens of thousands of dollars."

"For a book?" Sam nearly choked on her tea.

"My dear, yes. Rare books can hold very high values, especially if they were signed by a famous author and are in new condition. This was neither, I'm afraid."

Still ... Sam thought about it later, as she said goodbye and got in her truck. People tended to hang onto the most juicy part of any conversation. If one of the Chocoholics walked away from that meeting believing Rupert owned a book worth several thousand dollars ... well, people had been killed for a whole lot less.

Chapter 10

Rupert's revelation about the book stayed with Sam. She'd planned to go home and relax on her day off, but she knew her mind would never settle down. If she dropped this new information on Beau—the fact that the book might have been valuable and therefore a motive— he would deal with it. She could skim through a bit of housework and then settle in with the novel she'd tried to start a week ago.

The sheriff's department offices were on her way, so she turned onto Civic Plaza Drive and looked for a parking spot at the curb. During weekdays they were a precious commodity but today she found one near the department's small parking lot. She pulled her coat tighter against the November morning chill and walked toward the building. The first person she spotted was Beau. He and a man in mechanic's coveralls were examining a cruiser in the parking lot, presumably Beau's vehicle that had been taken by the naked guy during the Halloween hijinks last night.

He signed some piece of paper on a clipboard and sent the other man on his way. Sam told him about her visit with Rupert as she walked with him to the back door of the squad room.

"Interesting," he said. "It would be good to have at least a ballpark idea what that book is really worth. Too bad it's gone."

"I could ask Ivan about it tomorrow. He's the only person we know who's experienced with books and actually handled it. He may have resources he can check and get an estimate for you."

"Good idea." He pressed a keypad beside the door and opened it, standing aside while she walked in.

"We're interviewing the widowed man, Keith Trawl, this morning. Usually, when we see people in his situation they're in shock, having a hard time concentrating on our questions and fuzzy about details because their focus goes entirely toward the realization their spouse will never be home again."

"Usually? You mean he's not like that?"

"Kind of yes, kind of no … He doesn't seem to be all that broken up about Darlene's death. I mean, he is in a way. But in other ways, I sense this was not a complete surprise."

"You think he might be the killer."

His eyes narrowed as he put his thoughts together. "Can't really say that either. Something's just *off* about his demeanor. We'll figure it out. Rico's with him now. Part of the problem is he seemed to be right there in the crowd the whole time. He was dressed as Sherlock Holmes—yes, there were three or four of them—but this one's presence appears to be accounted for. I'll need to re-interview some of the other partygoers and see if everyone is in agreement on that point.

"Meanwhile, I want to look closer at the victim's background. You wouldn't be up for some online research, would you?" He unlocked the door to his office. "You don't have to—I know it's your only day off."

Sam felt torn. As much as she looked forward to a vacant spot on her calendar, she knew she wouldn't concentrate on a novel with all this going on. If she could help Beau, he might get away earlier and it would give them some time together.

"Sure," she said. "Point me toward what you need."

He pulled out his desk chair and signed onto his computer with his department password. "Start with social media and a basic Google search. It's amazing how much information people share online for the whole world to see. See if she had a Facebook page or Twitter account. If she talked or posted anything about hobbies, travel, other interests outside the ones we know about—those things could be useful. I want to compare what we can learn on our own with what the husband is saying."

She took the chair, sat, and smiled up at him. Social media was not at all her thing, but she could figure it out. He told her he was heading back to the interrogation room and would check back. If she was up for lunch at their favorite taco place later, he'd buy.

The lunch offer brightened her mood. At least she and Beau would have part of their Sunday together. She started searching for Darlene Trawl's name.

Google turned up way too many results, mostly for people far from Taos; the only relevant-seeming one showed Darlene had a Facebook page. Sam clicked over to it and discovered she would have to put in a Friend request and be approved by Darlene before she could view things posted. Well, that wasn't going to happen.

It did indicate most of the Chocoholics were Darlene's friends, along with others interested in books, gardening, and the Wicca Society. Hm, now that might be a possible connection. It could at least explain why Darlene chose to come to the party as a witch rather than a specific literary mystery character.

Sam's encounters with local Wiccans were limited, mainly when one of them wanted a cake. Her impression was they were more into nature, herbs and the spirits of woodland creatures than warty green faces and casting spells over cauldrons. Still, if Darlene had any interest whatsoever in the occult it could explain why she'd latched onto Rupert's old book.

She performed another search, following the name of a local Wiccan society, but of course there was no membership list online. The website blog talked at length about extensive study before one could practice magic and advised that a witch should never try a spell without knowing exactly what she was doing. She took down the name of the woman who wrote the blog. If there was a phone listing, she might be able to get information with a call.

Sam supposed there might have been some sort of witchy intrigue underway that led a member of the coven to go after Darlene. Still, it seemed a little farfetched. Seriously—if a witch wanted to kill someone wouldn't she do it with a spell in the forest rather than a knife in a public place? The book seemed a tentative lead for a motive. Otherwise, it was hard to fit those particular pieces into the puzzle.

Beau looked in on her. "Ready for a break? You've been at it two hours."

Her eyes went to the clock on the computer. Wow. Her stomach growled, reminding her about his promise of lunch.

They got into his cruiser, which smelled heavily of disinfectant with undertones of something a little more visceral. He powered all the windows down and Sam refused to let herself contemplate details about the vehicle's past twenty-four hours.

Paco Taco was jammed with people when they arrived. Although the sun shone in a bright blue sky, the thirty-some degree temperature wasn't exactly conducive to sitting at the outdoor tables. Sam spotted a young couple with two kids making moves to leave so she claimed their spot by the front window. Beau went to the counter to order their usual: chicken tacos for her, beef for himself, and a couple of soft drinks.

"Anything of interest turn up during your online search?" he asked as they settled down with their food.

Sam told him of the Wiccan connection and her idea that it might have spurred Darlene's interest in the old book. "If I can get hold of this woman who writes the local blog and *if* I can convince her to share names with me—which I'm not at all sure about—we might spot someone who was also at the party. It's the only way I can think there's a reason someone would want to kill Darlene and steal the book."

Beau nodded thoughtfully but she could tell he didn't quite agree with her conclusion. Before she could ask him to share his thoughts, a familiar voice called out.

"Hello again," said Rupert. "Might I join you two? Tables are at a premium right now."

Beau gestured toward an empty chair, and Sam guessed he'd been wanting to talk to Rupert anyway.

"We were just talking about your missing book," Beau said. He lowered his voice to avoid being overheard. "How it might have been the real motive for the person who attacked Darlene."

Rupert unwrapped a very large burrito from its protective paper. "Of course, there was one other small thing—our witch actress deviated from the script somewhat. At the moment the lights went out, I should have been the one holding the book."

"Really?" A pang of worry shot through Sam. First Zoë, now Rupert? She found herself speaking quietly, too. "Who would have known this? Was anyone else familiar with the script?"

"No, no one. I've thought about it quite a lot—whether I might have been the intended victim—but I simply don't see how. There would have been much easier ways to get at me, or to get the book. Going after it at a party was … well, it had to have been spontaneous."

"And yet someone came prepared with a weapon and was ready to act very quickly," Sam said.

She glanced toward Beau who was chewing and thinking.

"Another thing came to me," Rupert said. "We never did a thorough search of the bookshop. We are assuming the book was the motive, but what if it wasn't? What if the killer had another reason entirely for going after this woman?"

"We can't rule out anything," Beau said. "Remember, we're still very early in the fact-finding phase of the case."

The way he said it, Sam knew there were other things on his mind, facts he couldn't reveal to Rupert, perhaps things he couldn't even tell her.

They quickly finished their lunch and said goodbye to Rupert. They'd no sooner reached the cruiser than Beau's phone rang.

"Hey, Lisa. What've you got for me?" He listened a moment and said he was on the way.

Sam looked at him.

"Initial crime scene reports are coming in. The good news is they found the murder weapon. It was in the dumpster behind your bakery."

Chapter 11

Sam digested the news along with her tacos, which weren't settling very well at the moment. Not that she suspected anyone she knew would purposely throw a bloody knife into her trash receptacle, but having her business associated with the crime was a complication she didn't need.

"Can I come along to see what Lisa says?" she asked as Beau pulled into his normal parking slot.

"Absolutely. And later I'm going to have you and Rico head the team to search the bookstore for the missing book."

She trailed him through the back entrance and spotted Lisa with a box of evidence-bagged items at one of the squad-room desks. They'd met on several previous occasions and Lisa greeted Sam apologetically.

"Sorry I interrupted your Sunday lunch. Crime never takes a break, it seems, and I thought the sheriff would need to know about this."

"No, it's good you called."

Beau reached for one of the red-banded evidence bags. It contained a knife with darkened blood dried on it. The handle was brass, carved with ornate patterns, and the pointed blade looked sharp and deadly.

"We tested the blood and it's a match for the victim," Lisa said. "The length and shape are right, although if necessary we can send it to the OMI's office in Albuquerque to be absolutely sure it's the same weapon. It's at least a ninety-percent certainty."

"Prints?"

"None, I'm afraid. The texture of the handle would have made it difficult to get anything usable but there's not even a smudge. The killer must have worn gloves."

"Any sign of the gloves in or near the dumpster?"

"No clothing whatsoever," Lisa said. "And that's odd. With a wound of this type, there's no way the killer didn't get blood on himself. He or she either got out of the area without being noticed or they discarded the bloody clothing nearby and we haven't found it yet. You might want to put the word out for garbage collectors in the area to watch for it."

Beau didn't look happy. Sam knew automated garbage trucks with metal arms lifted dumpsters, tipped contents into the truck, set the bins back and moved along quickly. It wasn't as if a man watched the process close up. And multiple trucks covered this part of town.

"At least there's no trash pickup until tomorrow," Beau said almost to himself. "Maybe we'll catch a break yet today."

He thanked Lisa for the evidence reports and took the large box to his office. Sam followed along, thinking back over the previous evening. Offhand, she didn't remember seeing any costumes that included a knife. Gloves were common—the night had been chilly. There had been several in Victorian clothing and three or four in Sherlock Holmes attire. There was Count Dracula, Indiana Jones, Cleopatra … but she knew most of them and most did not have gloves as part of their costumes. There had been a Nancy Drew who almost certainly didn't wear gloves although her Ned Nickerson boyfriend could have had them. She remembered a Wyatt Earp, a Zane Gray, a definitely-ungloved Geronimo. Her head began to swim. Perhaps if they went back through Beau's and Rico's interview notes from the party.

As if he'd heard his name, Rico appeared at Beau's office door.

"Okay, Sam, if you don't mind I'm going to send you with Rico to meet your friend Ivan at his shop. There will be two other deputies with you, and the job is to comb the store top to bottom for that missing book. Rupert had a good point last night—the easiest place to hide a book would be in the bookstore. The killer wouldn't have wanted to be caught with it, so we have to cover this possibility before the murderer comes back for it or one of Ivan's browsers handles it. We need fingerprints intact if at all possible."

Finding fingerprints seemed remote, even to Sam. If the killer didn't leave prints on the knife he most certainly wouldn't have left them on the book.

Still, it was a vital piece of the case and they needed to find it. The sad part would be if the old book ended up in a dumpster somewhere and became a disintegrated scrap of trash by the time they located it. Damaged, the value of the book would most certainly plummet to zero.

Sam decided to take her own vehicle for the mission, hoping if they found the book quickly she could just scoot on home for the rest of the day, although she supposed she ought to check in with Beau since she was now on semi-official duty as a deputy.

Sam and Ivan opted to check the used book section, while another deputy searched the various new book categories. Rico and another man would go through the store itself, check the back room, under the platform stage, even go through paper towels in the restroom. Lisa and her assistant had already covered much of this ground but it was before the importance of the book was known. It couldn't hurt to check everyplace again.

The used books were shelved closest to the fateful stage area and it was where the old book would logically blend in. Easy access and easy disguise. Sam and Ivan were the only two in the search party who had actually seen the book. Sam began with high hopes; Ivan, not so much.

"I do not be liking this," Ivan complained under his breath to Sam as they started with the shelves closest to the spot where Darlene had died. "This thing—it can destroy business. And having police all over. Is distressing me."

"I know, Ivan. We all would have been better off if it hadn't happened." She ran a fingertip near the spines of the books, without actually touching them, to help focus on the titles. All she remembered about the cover was that it was brown.

Rico and his helper stepped in behind Sam and Ivan and began pulling the carpet cover from the wood stage.

Seeing the dried blood once again reminded Sam of the serious nature of the investigation. Even though she hadn't known Darlene Trawl she felt a pang of sadness over the whole situation. The wooden planks made scraping sounds across the floor as the men disassembled the stage and moved the parts to the back room.

Ivan kept his eyes on the books, avoiding the deputies altogether. Sam wondered whether his demeanor had to do with his past or if he was just pissed that his party had gone so badly off track. It had started out as such a fun evening.

They covered half the shelves and walked across the open space where the stage had stood, now facing the rest of the used-book shelves. It reminded Sam how often Beau had told her most of his job involved routine and pure boredom. Only a small fraction of his time saw much action. As a wife she appreciated that; as a deputy she was thankful she didn't have to do this day after day. Baking and decorating cakes had its own certain routine but at least it was creative and her customers provided a lot of variety to the workday.

"How's it coming over there?" she called out to the deputy who was skimming through the shelves of paperbacks.

"No sign of anything old over here," he said. "Well, except maybe this paper plate with cheese dip that didn't get thrown out last night."

The chuckle lifted all their spirits a little.

It was nearly five o'clock by the time they declared the entire store well and truly searched. But no spell book, not anywhere. The three deputies got into their car. A quick stop to clock out and they would be free for the evening.

Sam sat in her truck and watched Ivan lock the store and wave goodbye as he pulled out of the parking lot. She called Beau and briefly reported their lack of results.

"Looks like the killer thief did manage to get the book out of the store. Remember, I mentioned discovering Darlene's interest in Wicca and the local woman who blogs about it? If it's okay with you I'll give her a call, see if she's heard of this book. Then I'm on my way home—unless you need me back at your office?"

He said he'd been going back through the party crowd interview transcripts all afternoon and assured her he was more than ready for the day to end.

Sam found the note she'd made with the woman's contact information. Autumn Feather's real name was Cleo Patterson and it had only taken the department dispatcher a few minutes to come up with the right number. Sam dialed it.

She hadn't actually considered what approach to take, and when Autumn Feather answered on the first ring, Sam just blurted out what she was after.

"I read some of your blog online today and I have a question. Are you familiar with a book called *Spells and Incantations For the Proficient Witch?*"

"Who is this?" asked a mellow voice with an inquisitive edge to it.

"Sorry." Sam introduced herself, mentioning she had recently met Darlene Trawl and learned of Darlene's interest in Wicca. She left out the parts about the murder and how she was really asking on behalf of the sheriff's department.

"And she told you of this book?"

"Well, we were looking at a copy of it—"

"Here? In Taos? You saw a copy of that book here in this town?" The formerly gentle voice became forceful.

"You seem surprised."

"Ms. Sweet, that book is extremely rare. There probably aren't a dozen copies in the whole world. Any real witch would kill to own one."

Chapter 12

Sam hung up before Autumn Feather could pry any more information from her. It should be the other way around—she knew this—but she felt suddenly out of her depth. She wasn't sure what Beau could do about it at the moment, but she had to pass the witch's statement along to him. She drove home mulling it over.

Ranger their black Lab and Nellie the border collie greeted her with their typical happy-dog excitement, tails whipping back and forth, bodies in motion. She knew the reason was more about getting their dinner than actual enthusiasm for her company, but it was a nice way to be welcomed home nonetheless. She patted their heads and spoke to them. After a day of murder investigation, their cheerful mood was a refreshing change.

The dogs followed her to the kitchen and before she

scooped kibble into their bowls she heard Beau's vehicle coming up the long driveway.

"Whew, I can't say I was unhappy to see this workday end," he said as he hung his Stetson on the rack near the front door and shrugged out of his jacket. "This case is a tough one. I guess it's mainly the fact we have so many people who had access to the victim, and with every one of them I have to sort out the real person from the character they played that night."

Sam sympathized. Aside from her close friends, the rest of the crowd was a blur of masked faces. She felt badly that she couldn't recall more of them but her attention had quickly focused on Jen, Rupert, Kelly, Scott and Riki, making sure those dearest to her were safe.

She got Beau a beer from the fridge and told him about her call to Autumn Feather, the Wiccan lady. "She actually said, and I quote, 'Any real witch would kill to own one.'"

Beau digested the new information. "If there are only a dozen copies known to exist, I can well imagine."

"You might want to add to your list of questions for the partygoers—ask whether they know anything about Wicca."

His indulgent smile told her he was a step ahead of her in that department. "While you were having a leisurely afternoon at the bookstore, I had a parade of the guest list coming through my office. I tell you, no one wanted to spend part of their Sunday at the sheriff's office."

"But they came anyway?" Sam pulled out a container of homemade green chile stew she'd planned to reheat for their dinner.

"They came anyway. I talked to most of the book group, at least. Learned one tasty little bit of gossip from your friend Riki." He stood with a hip against the counter, an open bag of tortilla chips at hand. "She says Darlene Trawl and Alan Pritchard were having an affair."

Sam stopped in mid-stride, trying to remember Pritchard. "Tall, good-looking guy? Dark hair? He was dressed as Max DeWinter from *Rebecca*, I think, and his wife is the leader of the book group."

"Wow, very good. I had forgotten his costume—or I had no idea who he was supposed to be—but I did remember the wife making some comment about him not appreciating chocolate enough."

"Hm, so Riki says he was having an affair with Darlene? I would not have pictured that." She set the soup pot on the stove and lit the burner.

"Unfortunately, I only learned this from Riki after I had already interviewed the Pritchards and Keith Trawl."

"Ooh, yeah, I can see a motive for Keith to have been furious with his wife. Maybe he had only recently learned about the affair."

"Riki says they kept it pretty discreet. She didn't want to tell us about it the night of the party with the whole group nearby because she didn't think many of them knew. She thinks it had been going on for at least a few months."

"I wonder how Riki figured it out."

"She says she saw them coming out of a vacant house one afternoon. Alan's in real estate and it was his listing. When she said hello Alan turned the other direction and Darlene turned white as a sheet before coming up with some lame excuse. Well, in Riki's own charming British way, she said it came out as 'pure bollocks'."

Sam mulled over this new bit. "So, this makes me wonder … could the affair and the valuable book somehow be a common link here? Or do you have two separate crimes to solve?"

"I suppose Darlene's jealous husband could have known of someone who wanted the book. It may all come down to figuring out who switched off the lights at the opportune moment."

The answer to the question came sooner than either of them expected when Beau's phone rang at seven o'clock the next morning. Sam had let Julio take over opening the bakery, giving herself a few extra hours to sleep late and have breakfast with her husband.

"Yeah, Lisa," Beau said when he saw the phone's display. He tapped the speaker button, leaving his hands free to butter his toast. "What's up?"

"Sorry to bother you this early. I have a court case later and was afraid I wouldn't catch you at the office. Wanted to let you know I've identified a good, sharp fingerprint from the switch plate at the back door of the bookstore. It's a match to one of the party guests, a Keith Trawl. By the name, I'm guessing he's related to the victim?"

"Okay, very good. Were there any others?"

"Ivan Petrenko's. We took his prints at the store for elimination, since he's touched everything in the place. Otherwise, only the usual smudges that could belong to anyone."

He thanked the crime scene tech and hung up.

"The mystery club would say the plot thickens," Sam said.

"Or narrows. Looks like we're homing in on both motive and opportunity, but we can't come to a conclusion until we rule out a few other things."

"The spell book."

"Right." He swabbed his toast into the last of his egg yolk, popped it into his mouth and carried his plate to the dishwasher. "I'd better go. Did you give me the name and phone number of the witchy lady you spoke to? In case I need to get more information on the rarity of the book."

Sam looked it up on her phone's list of recent calls and read it off to him. They walked out the door together, Beau going to his cruiser and Sam to her bakery delivery van.

Her shop smelled of pumpkin and cinnamon when she walked in. Julio was pulling a tray of pumpkin spice cookies from the oven.

"Make sure we start the pumpkin cheesecakes today, too," she reminded. "By early afternoon we'll have people asking for them."

"I'm on it, boss," he said. "I already baked the *Dia de los Muertos* cookies." He nodded toward a cooling rack full of skull-shaped sugar cookies.

The tradition, brought north from Mexico, never failed to entice adults who prepared treats and flowers to honor family members who had passed on. The decorated cookies were a favorite with kids as well, Sam suspected mainly because of the appeal of the skulls themselves. She had seen elaborately decorated sugar skulls done in the Mexican tradition but had to restrain herself with embellishments. A cookie, no matter how beautifully done, could only bring a certain price and she wanted these to be affordable for the school kids who dropped by each afternoon with a little spare change in their pockets.

Becky arrived and started to make sugar flowers for a wedding cake due Friday. This one called for fifty peonies in varying shades of pink, and the flowers would need time to set up before they could be placed on the fondant-covered tiers.

"I saw a dress in a magazine," Becky said. "It had this ombré effect with pink chiffon layered from a deep rose pink at the top to almost-white—just barely a hint of pink—at the bottom of the skirt. The idea popped into my head to try that with the cake." She held her hands up, indicating.

"See? The flowers will be dark up here … a little lighter … lighter still … very pale here," she finished, her hands at the level of the bottom tier.

Sam looked up from the skull cookies. "Sounds fabulous—go for it."

Thirty minutes later, a tray of decorated skull cookies and another filled with Julio's thick triple-chocolate brownies were ready. Sam put her decorating tools aside and carried the cookies to the display case, her excuse to check out the crowd. All bistro tables were full, customers enjoying their coffee and newspapers, a trio of office ladies taking a final few minutes to chat before they had to report to their jobs.

Movement in the parking lot caught her eye. Beau's cruiser stopped in front of Ivan's bookstore and her handsome husband got out.

"I'm going to walk over and see what's up," Sam told Jen. For the first time in two weeks she didn't have a pile of urgent orders demanding her attention. Plus, she'd found herself unable to stop thinking about the weekend's events.

"Hey, pretty bakery lady," Beau teased when she emerged from her shop. He deposited a light kiss on top of her head. "Are you swamped with work or do you have time to give me a hand?"

"Now's a great time." She followed him into the bookstore.

Alex stood behind the counter. One of the cats had draped itself over the computer monitor and the other sat in the middle of the desk.

"Edgar and Agatha love to be in the middle of the action," the girl said. "Sorry Ivan's not here yet. He had a rough weekend."

"We were here," Sam said.

"Oh, yeah, that's right. It got pretty crazy."

"I need to measure something," Beau said. "We'll be in the back room."

He headed that direction, not giving Alex a chance to protest, and Sam followed.

"Okay, what I'm trying to get into my head is whether it's feasible Keith Trawl switched off the light and made it all the way to the stage and stabbed his wife in the short time while the lights were out."

The stage itself had been dismantled and put away yesterday but the floor space sat empty and most of the folding chairs the audience used were sitting a little helter-skelter in the same area they'd been Saturday night. It still gave a fairly good idea of the layout.

They walked through to the back room and Beau headed for the light switch on the far wall. Mimicking the flipping of the switch, he strode quickly through the doorway and into the stage area.

"You'd better time me," he said.

Sam kept track of her watch's second hand as he repeated the moves, lingered 'on stage' for a few moments, then dashed back.

"Fifty-seven seconds," she said.

"Most of the partygoers seem to be in agreement the lights were out for about a minute. That can seem like a long time when you're sitting in the dark."

"I'd say it's about right," Sam said. "It looks possible—for Keith to make it from the back door to the stage and back again—but the timing would have to be absolutely perfect. What if he had stumbled or tripped? What if Darlene had moved in the dark and he didn't immediately get to her?"

"Yeah, it's a problem. The audience chairs are actually a lot closer. Puts us back at square one. Anyone in the front row and most anyone else who was ready to move quickly could have gotten there sooner than Keith."

"Maybe he was in cahoots with someone else? They had it planned where he would switch off the lights and the other person would dash up to the stage. There were some thumping sounds and a crash," Sam said. "But it would take a lot of coordination between them."

"Not to mention keeping the secret as each was interrogated separately. Most people can't pull that off. One will cave. And we still have the problem of the killer's clothing being covered in blood." He eyed the distance again and did a couple more practice runs. "It's not impossible. Be interesting to see the reaction when I talk to Mr. Trawl again, won't it?"

Chapter 13

Sam kissed Beau goodbye at his vehicle before she went back to work. Becky had made good progress with the sugar peonies, so Sam picked up a different order and started to work on a birthday cake for a woman whose hobby was quilting. The daughter had provided a photo of a complicated quilt design and wanted Sweet's Sweets to duplicate it on a cake.

As Sam worked to cut bits of fondant into small squares and triangles for the quilt design she thought about the theory she and Beau just tested next door. Something about the scenario didn't feel quite like the right answer.

Even though Keith Trawl could have managed to switch off the lights, dash through the storage room and onto the stage, she wasn't a hundred percent convinced he did so. The book was the stumbling block. Why would a man who killed his wife in a jealous rage take the time to remove and hide the book she'd been holding in her hand? He'd gone to some effort to take it completely off the premises and it didn't quite add up.

When she reached her limit with fondant quilt squares she decided to follow up on the aspect of the case Beau hadn't found time for: chasing down the witchy leads on the valuable book. She hung up her baker's jacket and told the girls she would be out for awhile.

Her first conversation with Autumn Feather hadn't netted much information but she was determined to be ready with better questions this time around. She found the address online, under the woman's real name, Cleo Patterson, and discovered she lived partway up the road to the ski valley.

Twenty-five minutes later, Sam followed a two-track driveway up to a munchkin-sized log cabin with window boxes of herbs and a large woodpile beside it. Ponderosa pine forest surrounded the little structure on three sides, leaving a clearing with a fairly new blue Prius in it and just enough space to turn a vehicle around. She parked her bakery van beside the Prius and got out at the same moment the front door opened.

The doorway framed a surprisingly large woman. She wore a loose black tunic and pants, and some type of amulet hung on a cord around her neck. Sam found herself momentarily imagining whether someone of this person's girth would be comfortable in such a small home. Silly, she knew. People often chose places that felt cozy to them.

"Are you Autumn Feather?" she called out.

"I am. Welcome." When she smiled, the woman's round face took on a peaceful, gentle attitude. Her long salt-and-pepper hair flowed to her shoulders, creating the impression of a pyramid atop a cube.

She stepped onto the porch and beckoned Sam forward.

"I'm Samantha Sweet. I spoke with you briefly on the phone yesterday."

"Yes, I know."

Sam realized the witch was looking at the bakery van, which was covered in an eye-catching graphic design of pastries and had the name Sweet's Sweets prominently displayed.

Autumn Feather looked skyward, appreciating the deep blue midday light, then turned her attention back to her guest.

"Would you like to come inside? Since our conversation, I heard the news about Darlene Trawl. I assume that's what you want to talk about?" She stepped aside as Sam mounted the two steps leading to a narrow, covered porch. "Are you here because of an interest in the book you mentioned, or is this visit on behalf of the sheriff's department?"

"Is your information divinely inspired?" Sam asked. "Or am I somehow broadcasting my connections?"

Autumn Feather smiled again. "I may be a nature lover and I may live a somewhat remote woodland life, but I do keep track of the news. I also know many people in this town. It's no secret you are Sheriff Cardwell's wife and you've helped him on several cases."

"You *are* well-informed," Sam said, following her hostess's lead into a roomy central space that belied the cabin's exterior dimensions. "And, to answer your question, I suppose it's a little of both. I won't deny I plan to report anything useful to my husband. But I have to say this book fascinates me more with every new fact I hear about it."

Ms. Feather led the way to a pair of large, padded recliner chairs facing a stone fireplace where cheery little flames crackled. A pot of tea and two cups sat on the small table between them. Without asking, she poured.

"Is divination one of your skills?" Sam asked with a smile toward the teacups.

"Ah, I would like to think so, but in this case I heard your vehicle at nearly the same moment the kettle whistled. It's very quiet out here and I thought company would be nice."

The tea was a delicate Chinese oolong and Sam had to admire Autumn Feather's facility for brewing it perfectly. Sam sipped it as she blatantly scoped out the woman's home. The main room held a row of cupboards, narrow refrigerator and two-burner stove along the north wall. A doorway led to another space, presumably a bedroom since there was no evidence of a place to sleep in this one.

"Since we are aiming for full disclosure here," Autumn Feather said, "I will admit I feigned surprise when you mentioned the book to me yesterday. I had already heard rumors about a copy somewhere nearby. Both Darlene and Pete Winters had, in fact, spoken of it recently. You merely confirmed the story for me."

"Pete Winters?"

"He and Darlene move in common circles, both members of the same reading group and both with an avid interest in rare books. He's a collector and was hoping to find out who owned the spell book and whether they would be interested in selling it."

Sam vaguely remembered Pete, a guy in his thirties who seemed to have spent the entire Halloween party mooning after Riki. Who would have thought he knew anything about rare books?

"You said any real witch would kill for that book."

Autumn Feather rested her teacup on the arm of her chair and ran her other hand down the length of her black-clad thigh "I'm sorry—it's a figure of speech and I blurted it out without thinking. I am Wiccan. We live a life of peace and harmony with nature, a oneness with the Divine and all which exists."

"But—"

"Wiccans are witches but not all witches are Wiccan. You might compare it to other religions—while all Methodists are Christians, not all Christians are Methodists. There are differences in beliefs and practices everywhere, and I understand some of those others in witchcraft lean toward the dark side."

"And a spell book? How does that fit in?"

"A Wiccan spell book would contain healing potions—for relief of a headache, for instance. We use natural remedies and believe in love and harmony in all things. Other branches of witchcraft use other things. I cannot begin to tell you what the others believe—I have not practiced those beliefs."

Sam got the feeling asking more questions would only return the answers full-circle, with nothing new to be gained. She let the elements of the conversation tumble through her mind as she finished her tea.

When Autumn Feather showed her to the door, Sam turned.

"One favor, if I might," she said. "If anyone else asks about the spell book or if you hear anything about its current whereabouts, would you let me know?"

She pulled a business card from her backpack purse and handed it over, realizing it was probably a silly move. Autumn Feather seemed always to be a step ahead of her. Surely the Wiccan could easily find Sam if she wanted to.

Chapter 14

Interesting woman, Sam thought as she drove back to town. Although the practice of various forms of witchcraft wasn't uncommon—in fact, the woman who had given Sam her carved wooden jewelry box was rumored to be a *bruja*—she always learned something new when she encountered one. Mainly, a name had come up and Sam wanted to check it out.

Pete Winters. Fascinating about his interest in the old book of spells, especially since he'd become flustered at the party when Beau questioned him about having a knife as part of his Sherlock Holmes costume. And that huge overcoat—it had fabric enough to conceal a book deep within a pocket, if the man had been so inclined.

Now she knew Pete had known about the book's value

in advance and had gone so far as to talk with Autumn Feather—and maybe other witches—before the party, Sam found herself eager to share the news with Beau. She drove directly to his office.

She made her way to the squad room, where Rico sat at a typewriter, filling out forms from his interview notes.

"He's questioning Keith Trawl again," Rico said. "You can watch from the observation room if you like."

She supposed her news could wait. Rico unlocked the door to the small room which held monitors and recording devices to capture what was going on behind the mirrored wall in the interview room.

"Here you go," Rico said, flipping a switch so she could hear the conversation in the other room. "Would you like some water or a soda?"

"No, thanks. You've got lots to do."

He smiled gratefully and closed the door. Sam turned her attention to the room where Beau sat with his back to the mirror, giving their suspect little choice but to face the window and the camera.

"How often do I have to say this, Sheriff? I hit the light switch by mistake. I'd told Darlene I would meet her backstage as soon as the performance was over. She kept griping about her rubber mask, saying she didn't want to wear it very long and didn't want to carry it around all evening. I'd told her I could take the mask and anything else she wanted to be rid of and put it out in our car. I reached for the wall switches, thinking if I turned off the back room light it would be less distracting from out front. By that time I was dying to take a whizz and I dashed into the restroom."

Beau let four beats go by. "So you didn't hear what was

going on out front?"

Trawl shook his head.

Beau backtracked. "Why meet your wife in that room?"

"Hell, I don't know! Women—she just wanted to be back there when she took off the mask. Probably didn't want to look like a mess in front of *certain* people."

"Alan Pritchard?"

"Mainly him. I told you that before, too. I found out about the two of them and learned it's been going on awhile."

"Must have made you pretty angry," Beau said. "Maybe angry enough to kill, I'd guess."

Keith glared at him. "You know what? I'm done with this. Next time you want to talk it'll be at my lawyer's office." He stood quickly, nearly tipping over the metal chair in which he'd been sitting.

Beau slammed his hand down on the table-top and Sam jumped. "You have the right to an attorney, Mr. Trawl. Call him if you wish. But this is a murder investigation and I'll say when and where the discussions take place. Got that?"

Trawl flinched at the unexpected vehemence. "Fine. But unless I'm under arrest, I need a break. I have cooperated with you people but now I'd like to go home."

From the set of his shoulders, Sam knew Beau had to show the guy who was in charge. He made Keith sit down while he flipped through his notes for a minute, then told the suspect he could leave.

"Stay nearby, though," Beau cautioned. "We're not done."

Beau gathered his papers as Sam watched. Discouragement showed on his face when he stood and glanced at the mirror. He always said the first forty-eight hours of a case were all-important and they were nearing that point without any firm breakthrough. Sam felt her heart go out to him. She left the observation room and met him in the hall.

"Hey, darlin'. What's up?"

"I got here a few minutes ago and Rico said I could wait here."

"Yeah, well, what did you think? Keith Trawl doesn't strike me as the type of guy who flips the wrong light switch and then waits a whole minute to turn it back on. There's something hinky about the whole thing, but I'm damned if I can figure out what's off. Meantime, he's going to get an attorney involved and I'll get nothing new out of him."

"I just had tea with a witch and there's some new information I can add to the mix," she told him. "Can we talk in your office?"

He led the way.

"Pete Winters," she said when she'd taken a seat in front of his desk. "What do you know about him?"

He paged through his interview notes as she related what she had learned from Autumn Feather.

"Did he say anything about Rupert's book? Because according to this Wiccan woman he definitely knew how rare and valuable it was. He'd been poking around and asking questions. So had Darlene."

Beau shook his head. "Nothing in here about the book at all. Most of the questions went toward whether there was a knife as part of his costume. I'd planned to ask him to show it to me but he swore Sherlock Holmes wouldn't have carried one."

"Just thinking out loud here," Sam said, "but what

if Pete and Darlene both wanted the book and were in competition for it? Darlene might have thought she could run off with it—especially if she had her husband backstage ready to turn off the lights. Pete sensed that's what she would do and decided he would stop her."

Beau drummed a pencil against the desktop, letting her run with her thoughts.

"Or … the two of them could have cooked up a plan to get hold of the book, sell it for the big bucks it was worth and split the money? I've been trying to picture the room as it was when the play started, imagine where everyone was sitting or standing. I *think* Pete Winters was near the stage, sitting in the front row as I recall.

"For that matter, Pete and Keith could have been in on it together. One guy wants to be rid of his cheating wife, the other wants a valuable item. What if Pete had the book in one of those huge coat pockets all along?"

"The theory about two people competing over a valuable book could be valid," he said. "People are weird—they'll kill for bridal gowns or sneakers, so why not a book? But we still have the problem that Pete didn't have blood on him afterward. Neither did Keith, but Keith did have access to the back door and could have rushed out."

"Okay, Pete didn't have time to change clothes. Keith did. He would have had to wear something over his party costume."

"A plastic rain suit or moisture repellent coverall would work. He could have gotten out the door, unzipped the garment and slipped it off, tossed it somewhere. Except we searched all the dumpsters in the alley behind the shops."

"There are trash receptacles all over the area. Including the Plaza shops, there must be nearly a hundred businesses within four blocks of my shop," Sam mused. "I wonder how long he was away from the party?"

Chapter 15

W"ell, I suppose there's no way around it," Beau said, groaning as he picked up the phone. "The deputies will hate me. We need to go through the contents of every garbage truck that collected from this part of town this morning."

He looked up a number on his Rolodex and dialed. "Hey, Rex. Beau Cardwell here. How's things in the trash business?"

The county landfill manager must have made some wisecrack because Beau chuckled.

"The trucks that picked up down here in the Plaza area this morning—when they dump their loads I need the area cordoned off. I'm sending my men out to search for evidence in a case—" His expression suddenly became sober. "Well, stop them! Don't bulldoze the area yet. I need a few hours out there."

Some more conversation from the other end.

"Okay. Good." He hung up and got out of his chair. "The fun begins," he said with a wry grin.

Sam didn't linger long in the squad room. She had a feeling the men would resent being given the nasty duties while the part-time deputy got off with computer searches and interviews, but that's the way it was. She was still wearing her bakery clothes, had a business of her own to run. She had already taken too much time off, and she'd given Beau the new info she'd gathered. She scooted out of there and returned to the challenge of piecing fondant into a quilt design on a cake.

The day passed quickly. It was fully dark outside and Sam had been home nearly an hour, holding dinner in the oven and debating whether to call Beau to check his plans. She was standing at the kitchen window, phone in hand, when headlights beamed across the driveway. From his expression as he got out of the cruiser and started for the front door, she knew it hadn't been a successful afternoon.

"Not a damn thing," he said when she greeted him at the door. "Nothing useful to us, anyway. You can't believe the stuff people throw away."

She stepped back. "Have a shower before anything else, then you can tell me about it over dinner."

Twenty minutes later they settled over plates of roast chicken with potatoes and veggies.

"All we can figure is unless some dumpster diver got to the coverall right away, Keith somehow managed to take it off, fold it carefully and carry it home with him. In the minutes after the crime, Rico only saw a distraught man whose wife's body lay in a pool of blood on the floor.

He only thought about getting the guy away from the distressing scene so he had an officer drive him home."

"I'm trying to remember what Keith's costume was," Sam said, tasting the potatoes and thinking they could use a little more salt.

"I didn't see the outfit. Rico said he was some kind of ogre or troll or something. Dark clothing that was big and baggy. A balled-up coverall could have been tucked in under it to create a large belly." He sighed. "I requested a search warrant for his property, but I'm not hopeful. He's had plenty of time to get rid of it."

"But he probably wouldn't have gotten rid of the rare book," Sam suggested.

"True. Tomorrow, I guess it'll be time to start calling back the rest of the party guests. Most of them got by with just a few basic questions, but now we know more and can ask for details."

He looked so tired Sam took pity and settled him in front of the TV with a bowl of ice cream while she did the dishes. When she came to collect his empty bowl he was dozing in the chair. With a gentle touch on the shoulder she roused him enough to climb the stairs while she locked up and turned out the lights downstairs.

On the master bath vanity Sam spotted her jewelry box and picked it up. Within a minute the dark wood began to give off its familiar golden light and she felt her hands warm. She set it in place and went to Beau.

"Let me massage your back and shoulders a few minutes," she said. "You look pretty achy."

"I am," he groaned. "I think I'm getting too old for field work that involves climbing around a smelly pit in the ground."

She admired his muscular back as she ran her hands over the skin, resting them in place so the warmth imparted by the box could seep into him. A few minutes into the treatment he moaned with pleasure.

"Be careful, you'll make me feel *way* better and I'll be ready to jump you."

"Big talker," she teased, although the idea had its appeal. "You were falling asleep in your chair ten minutes ago."

She continued to massage lightly and when he rolled over and began to unbutton her shirt she didn't complain a bit. Despite a long day for both of them, his kisses still worked their magic and Sam joined him under the covers. A half-hour later they fell asleep, blissfully entwined together.

Sam slept so soundly she didn't at first realize Beau had gotten up. She was surprised to see it was already after six when she heard him moving about in the bathroom. She joined him in the shower, reminding herself they hadn't had nearly enough couple time recently.

By the time she dried off and dressed and was rummaging for earrings in her jewelry box, his mind had gone back to his job.

"After everything we went through yesterday, this case is making me crazy with the lack of hard evidence," he said. "It looks like I'm back to interviews, which are frustrating because it's so easy for people to lie. But I'll review all the previous notes first and watch for contradictory answers. Someone knows something, and eventually they'll mess up and give information I can use."

Sam smiled at him. "You'll figure it out, honey. You always do."

He buttoned his uniform shirt over the Kevlar vest

they all wore nowadays. "I know you think the killing is closely tied with the book—and I'm not saying it isn't—but I think I need to go back to more basic motives. The marital problems between Keith and Darlene must figure in here somewhere. I'm going to talk to Alan Pritchard again. I wonder if Keith ever threatened him. For that matter, Alan may be the one person who would know if Keith had threatened Darlene."

"For a guy who was messing around with another man's wife, he was pretty calm and collected when you talked to him before."

"He was. He's definitely worth another conversation." Beau strapped on his belt and left Sam to finish dressing.

She stood at the bathroom vanity for an extra minute, resting her hands on the wooden box. It seemed this could very well turn into a day when she could use the extra energy and insight. If only the box could allow her to see one of those auras, or if she could spot invisible fingerprints as had happened on the first case where she had helped Beau.

Chapter 16

Becky's wedding cake of pink peonies stood tall and beautiful on the worktable when Sam arrived at Sweet's Sweets. The ombré effect was every bit as stunning as she'd described.

"Couldn't resist," Becky said. "I woke up early thinking about this one and had to get here right away to work on it."

"Nice dedication," Sam said with a smile.

She looked through her own stack of orders. There was a princess birthday cake for tomorrow. Sam had three popular standards she could practically do in her sleep and this particular customer had chosen one of those. A football theme for a little boy's party wasn't due until Friday afternoon. With Halloween in the past and Thanksgiving in the future, there wasn't much call for decorated cookies or cupcakes this week. Julio would concentrate on their seasonal specialty items, their signature pumpkin cheesecake, coffee cakes with loads of cinnamon and nutmeg and the apple-pear tart which had been a huge hit last year.

Sam took a breath and considered her earlier plan to leave the store in the capable hands of her crew and take a few days off. Before she could mention it the back door opened and Kelly walked in, dimpled smile in place and curls looking freshly styled.

"Hey, mama. How's things over here?" She looked longingly at the tray of apple strudel Julio was about to carry out to the sales room.

"Grab one quickly if you want it," Sam said. "They won't last long out front."

Kelly shook her head. "Nah, just wishful thinking. I'm trying not to outgrow all my clothes and it's a challenge now that I have a man in my life and we're eating out so much."

She held up her cell phone. "Thought I would pop over and show you some pics I took at the party the other night. If you have a minute."

"Sure." Sam set her order forms down.

Becky placed one of the darkest pink peonies on the cake and stepped to Kelly's side to look at the photos too.

"Okay, this is me and Scott right after we arrived. I got Ivan to take this one." Indiana Jones and Marion stood in a posed embrace.

"Now here's the food table. I wanted to get your all-black cake recorded for posterity but I think the lighting wasn't great. The picture doesn't look nearly as good as it did for real." She skipped past a couple more attempts at cake photos. "Oh, here are the guests arriving. I tried to get a bunch of them but with people I didn't know I only took pictures of the costumes I liked best. Isn't this blue Victorian outfit gorgeous? The lady told me she rented it from that vintage clothing place on Gusdorf Road. I would have loved to live back then and dress this way."

Becky murmured agreement.

"Then we have the witch up on the stage ..." Kelly flipped to the next picture on the phone. "Well, that's when the lights went out and I didn't get anything for awhile. Wait, I think I took a few more after the, uh, after the lady died. It got a little chaotic and people were bored standing around waiting for the cops. Mainly, these are friends. Oh, yeah, here's that fancy dress again."

Sam felt her eyes go wide, her heartbeat pick up.

"I need your phone," she said, grabbing it from Kelly's hand. "I'll be right back."

She caught a glimpse of Kelly and Becky standing in the kitchen with their mouths open as she dashed out the back door and got into her van.

Chapter 17

Sam felt her spirits soar. If she was right there was perhaps an end in sight, just when everything had felt confusing and bleak. For a second as she started her van, a vision of the carved box went through her head. Could her handling it this morning have somehow helped?

The beauty of a small town is the closeness of everything. Sam was at the costume shop on Gusdorf Road within ten minutes. When she showed the gray-haired woman at the counter the two photos, there was immediate recognition.

"Yes, dear, this second one. It's one of our nicer dresses."

The lady led Sam between racks of spangles from the 1920s and polka-dots from the '40s until she came to a wall of 19th century items. The blue Victorian dress hung in the midst of the selection. A plastic bag attached to the hanger held a pair of blue gloves. On the shelf above was the hat that went with it, the one with the purple ostrich feather.

The woman eyed Sam covertly. "I'm afraid I don't have one like it in your size. This one, I'm sure, would not be a good fit."

"It's all right, it's not for me." Sam took the hanger off the rack, verified it was indeed the same dress. She showed her identification. "The sheriff's department has an interest in this dress, pertaining to a current case. Can you tell me if the woman wearing the dress in the photos is the one who rented it?"

"Oh yes, I remember her well."

"Can you check your records and see when it was rented and when it was returned."

Sam followed the woman back to her sales counter where she picked up a paperboard box and lifted the lid. The receipt was near the top and she handed it to Sam. Amy Pritchard had used her own name and address for the transaction. It would give her an irrefutable alibi.

"When Mrs. Pritchard returned it, was its condition as it is now? Was it dirty or stained at all?"

"Oh, it was in perfectly fine shape. These vintage items often cannot withstand modern laundering methods so I use spot cleaning if there's a small stain. I only have them cleaned under the most gentle of conditions. This one required nothing of that sort."

Sam looked at the dress carefully. It could not have been worn during a stabbing, so somehow it had been substituted for the ruined dress. "I'm afraid I need to take it with me—the dress, its accessories and the paperwork. The department will give you a receipt and will return the dress when the case is closed."

The older woman dithered.

"Sheriff Cardwell can issue a warrant for it as evidence in a case but that will take time. I need for you to either loan it, rent it or sell it to me." She delivered the news with a pleasant smile.

The shop lady wrote out a receipt and told Sam she would like the dress back as quickly as possible. Sam walked out, happy to be able to deliver some hard evidence in the case, wondering how the next part of it would play out. The photos showed a subtly different skirt before the murder, but she still didn't know where the substitute dress—the bloodstained one—had come from or where it was now.

The short trip to Beau's office had never taken so long. She made a sharp turn into the parking lot labeled "Sheriff's Department Personnel Only." This time when Sam parked in the department's exclusive lot she didn't feel too guilty. Carrying the bagged dress gave her the feeling of having a little bit of clout. She pounded on the back door.

Rico came, looking puzzled even though he must have checked the peephole in the door first.

"Where's Beau?" she asked breathlessly, waving Kelly's phone in front of him. "This is the answer!"

Rico eyed the garment bag and the phone and blinked a couple of times quickly. "Um, well, he's interrogating one of the party subjects right now."

"Is it Alan Pritchard?" She started toward the interrogation rooms.

Rico nodded. He seemed torn between giving her free reign and asking for more details. "Uh, well, go ahead I guess."

A narrow vertical window gave Sam a glance into

interrogation room one, where she verified it was Alan Pritchard sitting across from Beau. Pritchard sat forward in his seat, hands clasped on the table, looking earnestly at the sheriff. She couldn't hear what he was saying. She shifted slightly, catching Beau's eye, signaling she needed to talk. He didn't look especially pleased.

Beau let Pritchard finish what he was saying before he stood up and excused himself.

"Sam? What's so important?"

They moved out of sight of the small window.

"Look at this." She brought up the pictures Kelly had taken. "Amy Pritchard before the murder … Amy after the murder."

Beau's eyebrows pulled together in front.

"The dress she's wearing afterward is different. She changed clothes." She held up the garment bag from the costume shop. "This is the *after* version."

He took the phone and paged back and forth a couple more times, a smile emerging. "Wow, Sam, good work."

"Giving credit where credit is due, Becky and Kelly helped me figure it out. Kelly told me Amy Pritchard said she'd rented her costume from a vintage clothing place."

He paced to the end of the short hallway and back. "Okay. Okay. Looks like Amy used the rented dress to establish an alibi of sorts. Most likely she returned the dress on time so she would have a receipt and a witness.

"I need to keep working on him," he said with a tilt toward the interrogation room. "Have Rico copy those photos off the phone."

She found Rico, who promised he would bring the phone back to her without erasing anything of Kelly's.

Chapter 18

Sam slipped into the interrogation room. Beau pulled out a chair for her and she noticed he'd draped the blue dress across the back of another, letting it silently call out for a reaction from the man across the table.

Pritchard gave it a glance, nothing more.

Beau restarted the conversation. "Go over it with me again, Alan. You were all set to leave your wife, and yet you agreed to attend the party together?"

Pritchard had undoubtedly been over this ground before; he sent an impatient eye-roll toward the ceiling.

"That's right. Darlene and I had been seeing each other for nearly a year. We were both in unhappy marriages and we fell in love. We planned to make a new life together. I informed Amy about a week ago. She became distraught—why, I don't know. She was no happier living with me than

I with her. My wife is a few years older than I am and I suspect she's reaching that desperation age, knowing it will be hard for her to find another man."

Sam wanted to laugh, or to slap him. The arrogance! She and Beau had met only a few years ago, and he was younger as well. It didn't necessarily follow that a woman over fifty would be desperate without a husband. Really.

"Even after that she wanted to attend the party with you?"

"She insisted on it. She'd made quite a fuss over having coordinating costumes so we would appear to be a perfect Victorian couple. She said it was the least I could do for her. Of course, she somehow convinced Darlene to dress as a witch—the irony was not lost on me."

Beau gestured for Sam to pick up the blue dress.

"Is this the costume your wife rented for the evening?"

Pritchard gave it a once-over glance. "I suppose so. Though I have no idea why she would rent something. She's got a closet full of old theatrical items from her Little Theatre days and chests of fabric from which she could have easily made something. I suppose charging an expensive item to my credit card was meant to act as a sort of final blow. I wouldn't be surprised to see a cruise or something equally extravagant show up next. She'll have her little revenge on me, I'm sure."

"Did you sit with Amy during the play?" Sam asked.

"Actually, no. I was near the back of the crowd. She got into a conversation with the best looking young man in the room and made her way to the row of seats nearest the stage."

"Where is your wife now?"

"Oh, I wouldn't be surprised if she is at home baking

my favorite cookies. She's become remarkably loving since Darlene—" His voice broke, one of the few scraps of emotion Sam had seen from him yet. "If Amy had acted this way the past ten years there would have likely been no affair."

Rico tapped on the door and stepped inside to hand Kelly's phone back to Sam. Beau stood and took the folder of photo prints from his deputy, speaking to him in a low voice. Sam wondered whether she should stay in the interrogation room or leave. While she waited for Beau's attention she paged through the party photos again.

"Oh, and Rico? Take this and have Lisa test it for bloodstains," Beau said, picking up the blue dress.

Alan Pritchard reacted. "Surely, you don't think—"

For the first time it must have dawned on him why Beau's questions were leading in the direction of his wife.

"I don't form conclusions until I have all the evidence," Beau said. "Sam? You have something for me?"

Excitement flushed through Sam as she figured out exactly what had happened. She tilted her head toward the door and they left Pritchard alone in the room.

"I don't think there will be any blood residue on the rented dress," she told Beau. "I had forgotten someone mentioning Amy Pritchard's theater experience, but Alan just now confirmed it. And she's an expert seamstress. Do you see? It all makes sense—Amy made a separate dress to cover the rented one. Theatrical clothing is often made with Velcro closures and easy methods to get out of something fast for quick changes backstage. She would have put on the theatrical version over the vintage dress.

"The dress is very similar but there are little differences." She brought up the photos again. "The overskirt, for one thing. The first picture has one—see the flounces that reveal a purple skirt underneath? The second one has the same blue everywhere. The gloves are blue fabric in the first one. They're gray lace in the second. She's carrying a little purse. I think she brought spare gloves in case she got blood on them."

Beau picked up her enthusiasm as she talked.

"She was in the front row and could easily get to Darlene. I'm guessing she got past Keith Trawl while he was in the bathroom, and she must have run out the back door. Then, out in the alley she could just rip off the damaged skirt and roll it up with the dirty side in, exchange the gloves, then rejoin the party."

"During the search, we didn't find any bloody clothing, remember?"

"She must have stashed it somewhere nearby. Risky, I know, but people do chancy things. She had to have done all this near the store so she could reappear pretending she'd been out for a smoke or to take a phone call or something."

"Well, there are some gaps," he said, "but the theory brings up some good questions for when she gets here. We'll pick her up. Meanwhile, maybe her husband can help us put a few more nails in her coffin, so to speak."

"I'll wait in the observation room," Sam said. "He might speak more freely if it's just you in there."

Beau left their guest alone for a few extra minutes while he visited the evidence locker. When he came back he dropped a plastic bag containing the murder weapon on the table in front of Alan Pritchard with a clunk.

"Recognize this?" he asked.

Pritchard blanched. To Sam, that seemed as if his reaction answered the question but Beau pressed and made him say it.

"It belongs with a collection of mine," the man admitted quietly. "I didn't even realize it was missing."

Chapter 19

Sam's cell phone rang down in her pocket, startling her. She glanced at the men in the interrogation room but apparently they hadn't heard it. The screen showed the call came from the bakery.

"Hey, Becky. Everything okay?"

"Fine at this end, but did you remember you were supposed to deliver this wedding cake today? I could do it, but you've got the van and it's a little too big for my car. They need it by noon."

Yikes. She'd forgotten all about it. "I'll be there in ten minutes."

Becky had braced the cake within a tall cardboard box and the two of them carried it to Sam's van.

"Here's the order form with the delivery address," Becky told her. "It's residential, a home reception."

Sam gave the page a glance. Something about the address resonated with her. She stared upward for a moment, thinking. The memory didn't arise from the customer's placing the order—she had seen this one only this morning. It was the address on the costumer shop's receipt.

A wedding at the Pritchard's home? That made no sense at all. The name on the order was Sanchez. She tapped the map feature on her phone and brought up the address. There was one quick way to find out. She hopped up to her driver's seat and started the van.

"Oh, Becky? Can you give Kelly's phone to her?" She handed the borrowed phone out the window. "I'm sure she's itching for it back—there are several texts from Scott."

Following the map directions, Sam found herself on Lilac Road within twelve minutes. It was a pleasant neighborhood, a mixture of adobe bungalows and territorial-style stucco homes. The few lawns had gone winter brown—most were landscaped with natural xeriscape plants and rock anyway—and there was a pleasant tang of woodsmoke in the air. The residence for the wedding party caught her attention. Golden globes and pink streamers decorated two tall spruce trees in the front yard, and a teenage girl with dark hair was in the process of tying a large bunch of pink balloons onto the mailbox at the curb. She looked up when she heard the vehicle and smiled at the sight of Sam's vividly decorated bakery van.

"Mom's going to be happy to see you!" she announced as Sam opened the back of the van.

The residence had concrete sidewalks, so Sam unfolded her wheeled cart and set the cake on it. Within minutes, she had the sweet confection safely inside and transferred to the prepared serving table. The mother of the bride beamed as she showed Sam to the door.

"I have to admit, I was a little confused when I saw your address," Sam said. "I know some people named Pritchard and thought they lived here."

"Right across the street," Mrs. Sanchez said. "It's the only adobe house with a red front door."

Sam stared toward the house, with its canopy of cottonwood trees and landscape of natural chamisa and river rock, as she stowed her cart in the back of the van. Alan Pritchard was at this moment talking to Beau. Where was Amy? Had she moved out already? Something Alan had said made Sam think not.

In one of those "think about it and it will appear" moments, a blonde woman emerged from a side door of the garage. She wore jeans and a sweater with an expensive-looking down jacket over it. Sam recognized Amy Pritchard and realized she was carrying a blue cloth bundle.

Sam's breath caught.

Amy moved furtively, cradling the bundle close to her body as she walked quickly toward a tall gate that must lead to the backyard. She hadn't yet looked in Sam's direction.

Sam closed the van's rear doors softly and watched as Amy lifted the latch on the wooden gate and slipped through. She pulled out her phone, ready to call Beau, but paused. What if the bundle was not the missing evidence? It could be anything at all, and Sam didn't want to disrupt the interrogation back at the office.

On the other hand, if the bundle did contain the blood-stained costume, Amy might be taking this opportunity while her husband was away to destroy it. If someone didn't

intervene quickly, the evidence would be gone forever.
The scent of woodsmoke sharpened.

Chapter 20

Sam felt the hair on her neck rise. She raced across the street, tackling the latch on the tall wooden gate. A concrete pathway led down the side of the house toward a flagstone patio and garden area. Two Adirondack chairs flanked a low fire pit where flames crackled in the chill autumn air. Sam took in the scene at the same time she hit her speed-dial number for Beau.

Amy stood beside the fire, a length of pine cordwood in her right hand, the blue bundle clutched in her left. She tossed the stick onto the fire, sending a rush of sparks skyward. The flames flared higher. When she began to unfurl her cloth packet, Sam knew exactly what was about to happen.

She sprinted toward Amy, an angry shout escaping as she ran. Amy turned, her mouth an O of pure shock, her eyes wide. She flipped the cloth and it billowed over the fire.

Sam reached out and shoved hard, sending Amy sprawling across the flagstones. Her phone fell into a nearby flowerpot as she grabbed desperately at the edge of the blue item. With a yank, she brought the cloth out of the fire. Flames licked at the garment in several places, trying mightily to take hold, to consume the fabric.

"What are you *doing*!" Amy shouted, ignoring her scraped hands.

Sam stomped madly at the slow-burning patches on the skirt, catching one spot, then another, putting them out before they fully took hold.

Amy let out a scream of rage, charging Sam, her claw-like fingers reaching toward Sam's face.

"How dare you!" she screamed. "This is private property!"

She hit with more force than Sam would have believed possible for such a skinny woman; they both went to the ground. Amy's nails grazed Sam's left ear before she could jerk her head aside. She responded with a knee toward the woman's gut, but the effort fell short and Amy skittered to the side, panting.

Sam rose, feeling slightly short of breath herself. She backed up, taking a wide stance, sizing up her opponent. Amy's eyes kept darting toward the blood-stained skirt on the ground, gauging whether she could get to it first. Sam side-stepped closer to the evidence, giving the other woman no chance to reach down for it.

"Give it up, Amy," Sam said, wishing her voice would come out a little more forcefully. "The sheriff has all the evidence he needs to arrest you."

Amy's glance toward the costume told Sam the woman still believed if she could get rid of this one item the law wouldn't be able to touch her.

"Your husband is there now, down at the sheriff's office. He's identified the knife used to kill Darlene. He says the knife belongs to a collection of his. It's been missing from your home since the day of the party."

"So?" Amy stood a little straighter, working to appear calm. "I'm surprised Alan would take one of his own knives and kill Darlene. The little skank wasn't worth the time."

"Alan didn't kill her. Amy, you and I both know it." Sam softened her expression. "It must have really hurt, the fact that your husband became interested in someone like Darlene Trawl. That must have left you devastated."

A twitch started near the corner of Amy's mouth.

"I mean, Alan's a good-looking guy. What would he see in someone who was content to come to a party as a witch? She just didn't strike me as really … um, *worthy* … of him."

Amy reacted to the snobby remark just the way Sam wanted her to.

"*Exactly*," she hissed through clenched teeth. "Alan and I were the perfect couple. Heads turned when we entered a room. I don't want to sound conceited but face it, we are a good-looking team. Who did Darlene Trawl think she was? The sneaking, conniving little bitch! Pretending to be my friend at the book club and then going behind my back to seduce my husband—she deserved exactly what she got. No one on this earth would blame me for striking out at her."

"This was a little more than a slap, Amy. You carried a deadly weapon with you. How did you get the knife there, in your purse?"

Her chin went up. "So what? I didn't plan to actually kill her. I knew if I used Alan's phone to send a text and ask her to meet outside she would do it in a heartbeat. Then I figured I could threaten her with just how easily a scar or two across her face could ruin her looks. If she was ugly, Alan would never go ahead with his dumb idea of leaving me and living with her. She would value herself over him. She would break it off."

"But that's not what happened," Sam said. "Did you and Keith make a plan together? He would turn out the lights and you could rush up to the stage in the dark?"

A cruel smile played across Amy's lips. "The lights going out was pure luck. I saw my chance and took it. Everyone in the room would be equally suspect. I'd already checked the layout of the shop because I planned to slip out the back door before sending Darlene the text message. I never saw Keith back there."

Sam changed tracks. "And the book? Why did you take it?"

She shrugged. "Who says I did?"

"Come on. It vanished at the same moment Darlene died—you want me to think someone else rushed up there and snatched it?"

"They were saying it was worth some money. There was that big guy, the one who brought the book in the first place. He could have easily taken it."

Sam swallowed. Rupert? Amy was implicating Rupert?

She caught movement behind Amy. When she realized it was Rico, she forced herself to keep her eyes on Amy as he made his way quietly toward them, a hand on his service pistol.

"Darlene really wanted the book, didn't she?" Sam

asked. "I'm betting you watched her from the moment you arrived at the party, and I'll bet you saw how interested she became when the book showed up. First Darlene wants your husband, then she wants a valuable book? You couldn't let her have either one, could you?"

Amy's lower lip quivered, but only for a fraction of a second. Rico stepped into her field of vision.

"Amy Pritchard, you are under arrest for the murder of Darlene Trawl."

Chapter 21

Rico showed Amy Pritchard to a chair in interrogation room two but she wouldn't sit. "Sheriff Cardwell will be right with you," he said, leaving the room. Sam knew when the door clicked shut it could only be opened from the outside.

From the observation room between the two interrogation rooms, she watched Amy pace the length of the small room twice, glance toward the mirrored wall. Guessing someone could watch from the other side, Amy gathered her composure and ran her fingers through her hair. Her down jacket had a rip in one sleeve and her slim-fit jeans were coated with dust. She removed the jacket and hung it over the back of the chair, brushed off most of the dirt, then sat and crossed her legs. One foot swung casually. Everything about her said, *I'm not worried about you people.*

Beau entered the room, carrying the file folder with the photos from the party and a yellow legal pad. The top sheet was blank but Sam knew he had pages of notes concealed beneath it.

"Look, I can play twenty questions with you, I can feed you a little information at a time, but you might as well go ahead and tell me what happened," he said to Amy. "I've had several hours with your husband and we know most of it anyway."

She glowered at him.

"We caught most of your conversation awhile ago with my deputy, Samantha. The minute I heard the scuffle over the phone, we began recording. Quite a confession you made there, ma'am. About the only thing you didn't fully answer for us was where you stashed the book."

Amy's cool deportment lasted until Beau left the room. Sam watched through the mirror, saw Amy couldn't conceal how much her hands shook as she lifted the top of the folder with the pictures. Beau came back in, carrying the blue dress and the bagged knife.

Amy tried the "those aren't mine" ploy for about a minute, but when Beau showed the rental contract for the dress and began to lay out the photos printed from Kelly's camera, a flicker of uncertainty played across her face.

"I want a lawyer," she finally said.

"Fine." Beau stood up and walked out of the room.

Sam heard his footsteps as he passed the room where she sat monitoring the recording equipment. He entered the other interrogation room where Alan Pritchard sat, exhausted by the long day.

Beau asked only one question: "If your wife had a very important item to hide, where would she put it?"

Alan blinked a couple of times. "How large an item?"

"A book."

He thought for a long minute. "Our house is adobe and there's an authentic *horno*, a bread oven in the back yard. We discovered a hollow space in the bottom. She once joked it would make a great jewelry safe. If you remove the bricks from the floor of the oven, you can get to the space below."

Beau left Pritchard alone and came into the observation room with Sam. "Looks like he's ready to hand his wife over to us. Did we get both interviews?"

She pointed to the ticking numbers on counters which indicated each camera was running. He smiled and pulled out his phone. He made a call to the judge's office, requesting a warrant, then told Rico to take another deputy and search the Pritchard place.

Sam's earlobe itched like crazy and when she reached up to touch it she remembered the wound Amy had inflicted. A glance in the restroom mirror showed her face and hair coated with dirt, her white bakery jacket beyond help. All at once she just wanted to go home.

Chapter 22

It felt like Christmas in the sheriff's department when Sam returned the next morning. Packets of bagged evidence covered one whole table in the squad room. Rico's search efforts had paid off hugely once they knew about the secret hiding place beneath the *horno* and the atmosphere was jubilant.

The search at the Pritchard residence had netted a pair of blue gloves with a substantial amount of blood on them under the backseat of Amy's car. The blue dress Amy had nearly burned up lay safely in an evidence bag now. The pieces had been constructed, exactly as Sam guessed, using Velcro closures and other methods for quick removal. The *horno* compartment held Rupert's book, *Spells and Incantations For the Proficient Witch*.

"He will be so happy to see this," Sam said, examining

the book through the plastic bag which contained it now. She pointed out a small torn place near the spine. "I hope the damage doesn't affect its value too much."

Rico pointed to another bag. "In the house there were remnants of the same material as the dress Mrs. Pritchard made. We brought all of it."

Beau had disappeared into his office for a few minutes. Now he announced the court was about to arraign their suspect for the murder. "I've also ordered the car she drove that night impounded. I feel sure it will give up enough evidence to tie all of this to the night of the party, just in case she tries some fancy semantics once she has an attorney."

Privately, Sam thought Amy had already cooked her own goose. She had talked way too freely yesterday, with the fire of indignation burning strong.

"I wonder why she tossed the knife into the dumpster, since she went to the trouble to hide all this other stuff," Sam said.

"It belonged to Alan," Beau reminded her. "In spite of everything she said about the two of them staying together with Darlene out of the picture, maybe she secretly hoped the weapon would lead us to her husband."

"Teach him a lesson?"

"Something like that," said Beau. "I imagine a psychologist could have a field day trying to figure out the logic of Amy Pritchard."

* * *

Midweek, and Sam felt a lull in her energy as she stared out the front windows of her shop and sipped her second cup of coffee for the morning. Low clouds had begun to build overnight and wispy snowflakes now floated through the air. Normally she would be baking an all-chocolate confection of some sort for the book club today but Ivan called yesterday to say they were not meeting again until further notice. Losing two couples from their close little band might end up being the death of the Chocoholics Unanimous group.

Despite handling the wooden box this morning she'd not received her usual energy boost from it; more likely it was sheer mental overload from the thousand bits of information coming her way during the interrogation and evidence collection at Beau's office. Even after she'd left to go home, her husband had paperwork to finish, the deputies were cataloging evidence, and the crime scene techs were going through Amy Pritchard's car with bright lights, tweezers and magnifying glasses. She wasn't sure how she handled the intensity of law enforcement—owning a very busy bakery felt mild by comparison.

A familiar Land Rover pulled into the parking lot, catching her attention. Rupert parked in front of Mysterious Happenings and walked into the bookshop with a wrapped gift in hand. Perhaps he'd taken pity on Ivan, who continued to bemoan the fact business had dropped off since Halloween night and news of the murder. Maybe she could help boost her neighbor's spirits too.

Sam set her cup down and stepped behind her display case of pastries. She chose a half-dozen of the prettiest cookies and most popular scones and muffins, placing the assortment into one of her purple bakery boxes and tying a bow around it.

To all outward appearances the bookshop was

returned to its former self. With furniture back in place, shelves dusted and attractively arranged and the two cats happily asleep on one of the forest green wingback chairs, the events of the past weekend melted away and the store welcomed all who entered.

Sam placed the bakery box on the counter near where Alex chatted with Rupert. "Ivan's just in the back," Alex said when she noticed a second gift. "I'll go get him."

Sam turned to Rupert once the store assistant had left. "So, all's well?"

"It was incredibly generous of Beau to give the spell book back to me before his case has actually gone to trial." He held up the wrapped package and Sam guessed the book was inside.

"There may not be a trial. Amy basically confessed on tape. It's going to depend on what her attorney advises. Even so, the murder charge will put her farther away than the theft of a book." Sam acknowledge the package. "You're giving it away? If it turns out to be worth something, it's a very generous gift."

"It's an item I don't need anymore. I've lost my yearning to write a story about witchcraft. I think the book can do more good for someone else."

"You think Ivan will want it?" Sam could hear the skepticism in her own voice.

"We'll see."

Movement at the front door caught their attention. Kelly and Riki came in together. Outside, Sam saw Zoë getting out of her car.

"Who's watching Puppy Chic?" Sam asked Riki.

"We put the Closed sign out for a few minutes. My first appointment isn't for another half hour," Riki said. "I have a little surprise for Ivan. Where is he?"

Zoë joined the group, giving Sam a hug and assuring them she was feeling much better since the weekend. From the wink that passed between them, Sam got the idea Kelly had invited Zoë to what was turning into an impromptu little party.

Voices came from the back, Alex coaxing her boss to come out. When he saw the bakery box and the group his face lit up.

"Is good to be seeing friends," he said, reaching out to touch hands here and there.

Rupert held out his gift.

Ivan took it tentatively and tore off the book-themed wrapping paper. His face paled. "You have received it back?"

"Let me say something before you decide whether you want it. I know this volume has unpleasant memories and it's not my intention to give you something to cause pain." Rupert reached into the inner pocket of his jacket. "Think of this as that game show on TV, the one where you may choose the gift you know or take the unknown behind the curtain. Except what's behind the curtain this time is in this envelope, and I will allow you to look at it before you must decide."

Everyone crowded around, eager to see what Rupert's mysterious game would turn into.

Ivan lifted the flap on the envelope and peered inside. Sam could see it contained cash.

"It's ten thousand dollars," Rupert said. "I contacted a friend of mine who is a dealer in rare books. With some detailed video footage of this book, he offered this sum. I want you to have it, Ivan, to get your store back on its feet and just *because*. I'm sorry my play ultimately caused such anguish. You may either accept the cash, in which case I will send the book to my friend, or you may keep the book and see if you can receive a better price by selling it yourself. The choice is yours." He set the envelope on the counter beside the book.

Ivan's lower lip quivered. He stared at the gift for a moment then threw his arms around Rupert's substantial middle. "Thanking you, dear friend! I thank you! Your friend is welcome to have the book and be selling it for big price."

Rupert smiled and lifted the smaller man off his feet for a second. Sam and the girls gathered around to congratulate and hug Ivan.

"I have a little surprise for you as well," Riki said, backing away and wiping her eyes. "Chocoholics Unanimous is revived. I have spoken with several people in recent days who would love to become members of our group. You know we have a little reputation, don't you? The book club for people who love mysteries and chocolates—everyone wants in. Confidentially, I believe Sam's pastries are the big selling point, although I've told them all that holding meetings at Ivan's store and purchasing the books from him is a requirement."

"It was Amy Pritchard who insisted the Chocoholics limit the size of the group," Kelly said. "I wanted to join a long time ago."

"Is wonderful news!" Ivan said, glowing as he put his envelope of cash away under the register. "And I have way to celebrate for us. Wait here."

As if anyone would immediately leave.

He returned with a bottle of champagne, which he

held up. "Was here for party. No one opened."

Alex came up with some small plastic flutes and Rupert did the honors of opening the bottle.

"To my good friends," Ivan said, raising his glass.

They all toasted.

Something had been weighing on Sam since the previous day. After her first sip of champagne she spoke up. "Amy Pritchard said something yesterday in the midst of a rant, something that made me realize the differences in people. She was so concerned with appearances, consumed with the idea she and Alan should be together because they *looked good* as a pair, not because they cared for each other or were happy together. It was sad to hear those sentiments."

Nods from the others.

"So, in addition to Ivan's toast, I would like to thank each of you for being my friend, to let you know you are an important part of my life."

"Hear, hear," said Rupert. He lowered his voice. "Truthfully, I will be glad to see this book go elsewhere in the world. Before I thought of contributing its value to a friend, I had considered hosting a large bonfire for it. But this is so much better. People are always more important than things."

So true. These people meant the world to her. Sam swallowed hard, blinked back the moistness in her eyes, and cleared her throat. "Let's eat those cookies!"

* * *

Author's Note:
Thanks for reading *Spellbound Sweets*. By now
you've figured out that I *love* everything about bakeries.
Check out my Pinterest boards, including "Cakes That
Inspired Me" to see pictures of the cakes I've used for
inspiration in my books. I invite you to visit my website
at **connieshelton.com** where you'll find some of my
favorite New Mexico recipes and discover my other
two mystery series, as well.

Sign up for my free mystery newsletter, too. There
are monthly prizes, along with background stories about
my books and characters, recipes and more!

* * *

Books by Connie Shelton

THE CHARLIE PARKER SERIES

Deadly Gamble
Vacations Can Be Murder
Partnerships Can Be Murder
Small Towns Can Be Murder
Memories Can Be Murder
Honeymoons Can Be Murder
Reunions Can Be Murder
Competition Can Be Murder
Balloons Can Be Murder
Obsessions Can Be Murder
Gossip Can Be Murder
Stardom Can Be Murder
Phantoms Can Be Murder
Buried Secrets Can Be Murder
Legends Can Be Murder
Weddings Can Be Murder
Alibis Can Be Murder
Holidays Can Be Murder - a Christmas novella

THE SAMANTHA SWEET SERIES

Sweet Masterpiece
Sweet's Sweets
Sweet Holidays
Sweet Hearts
Bitter Sweet
Sweets Galore
Sweets Begorra
Sweet Payback
Sweet Somethings
Sweets Forgotten
Spooky Sweet
Spellbound Sweets - a Halloween novella
The Woodcarver's Secret – prequel to the series

THE HEIST LADIES SERIES

Diamonds Aren't Forever
The Trophy Wife Exchange (early 2018)

Sweets From My Kitchen

Ten Family Favorite Dessert Recipes from Connie Shelton

Author of the Samantha Sweet and Charlie Parker mystery novels

Bonus Recipe Book

Sweets From My Kitchen

by Connie Shelton

* * *

To my mother and my grandmother, both excellent bakers, who lavished our family with these wonderful goodies.

Millionaire Pie (makes 2 pies)

My grandmother's recipe. We loved this pie when I was a kid, and my daughter still insists we have it every Thanksgiving and Christmas.

2 baked pie shells
2 cups powdered sugar
1 stick butter, softened
1 egg
1/4 teaspoon vanilla
1 cup heavy cream **or** 1 carton Cool Whip
1 cup crushed pineapple, drained
1 cup chopped pecans

Cream together powdered sugar and butter. Add egg and vanilla. Beat until light and fluffy. Spread mixture evenly into two baked pie shells. Chill. Whip the cream until stiff, fold in pineapple and nuts, spread over the sugar/butter mixture. Chill thoroughly before cutting.

Chocolate Nut Drops

Soft and cake-like, this was my very favorite cookie as a kid—and it still is! My mom has them in the cookie jar whenever she knows I'm coming to her house.

1 cup shortening
1-1/2 teaspoon salt
2 teaspoon vanilla
1-1/3 cups brown sugar
2 eggs, beaten
4 oz melted chocolate **or** 1/2 cup powdered cocoa
3-1/2 cups flour
1 teaspoon baking soda
1 cup milk
1 cup chopped nuts

Combine shortening, salt and vanilla. Add brown sugar and cream together well. Add beaten eggs, then chocolate. Sift flour and baking soda together and add alternately with milk. Stir in nuts. Drop by teaspoons onto a cookie sheet, sprinkle tops with sugar and bake at 350 for 10-15 minutes.

Easy Flan

Had this at a friend's house and thought, wow! It's definitely always a hit when I bring it to a potluck.

3/4 cup plus 1/4 cup sugar
3 large eggs
1—14 oz can sweetened condensed milk
1—13 oz can evaporated milk
1/2 teaspoon vanilla

Preheat oven to 325. Have a 9" pie plate or casserole dish handy. Pour 3/4 cup sugar into a warm pan over medium heat. Stir constantly until sugar melts and turns brown. Quickly pour the caramel-like melted sugar into the pie plate, swirling to coat the bottom. It will harden as it cools.

Blend eggs and milks with a whisk, then slowly mix in the 1/4 c. sugar, then the vanilla. Whisk until smooth. Pour mixture over the caramel in the pie pan. Place on cookie sheet to catch boil-over, bake about 1 hour 15 mins. Check for doneness when a knife inserted just to the side of center comes out clean.

When cool, invert onto a serving plate, if desired, and spoon the runny caramel over each serving.

Bizcochitos
(a traditional New Mexico Christmas cookie)

*A simple cookie, not too sweet, and the
cinnamon/sugar coating adds just the right touch!*

1/2 cup sugar
1 cup shortening
1/2 teaspoon anise seed
2 cups white flour
1 cup whole wheat flour
1/2 teaspoon salt
1 teaspoon baking powder
1/3 cup water (more may be added if dough is too
crumbly)
extra sugar and cinnamon for coating

Cream shortening and sugar together, beat until light
and fluffy. Add anise seed. Sift flours, salt and baking
powder together and add. Add just enough water to hold
the dough together.

Roll dough ¼" thick and cut with cookie cutters. Dip
each cutout in a sugar/cinnamon mixture and bake at
350 for 10-12 minutes.

Samantha Sweet's Red Velvet Cake

This is another recipe that I can't take credit for. It came from a dear writer friend, Sophie Dunbar, who, sadly, is no longer with us. I especially love her Original Icing recipe which follows:

Red Velvet Cake

1/2 cup shortening or unsalted butter
1-1/2 cups sugar
1 teaspoon vanilla
2 eggs
2 Tablespoons cocoa
1 Tablespoon white vinegar
2 ounces red food color
1 cup buttermilk
2-1/2 cups plain flour
1 teaspoon salt
1 teaspoon soda

1. Cream shortening, sugar and vanilla. Add eggs, one at a time, beating well.
2. Make a paste of cocoa, food color and vinegar. Set aside.
3. Mix buttermilk, flour, salt and soda. Set aside.
4. *Now!* Mix numbers 1, 2 and 3 together. Blend until batter is smooth.
5. Pour into 2 nine-inch or 3 eight-inch pans. Bake at 350 degrees F. for 40 minutes.

Original Icing for Red Velvet Cake

1 cup whole milk
5 Tablespoons flour
2 sticks salted butter
1 teaspoon vanilla
1 cup sugar

Cook milk and flour until thick in double boiler. Let cool. Cream sugar and butter in a mixing bowl. Add vanilla and blend until fluffy. Add cooled milk and flour mixture. Beat well.

[Note - this is a very soft icing, not suitable for piping decorations. But it is yummy!]

Coca Cola Cake

A very rich cake, super moist, and always pleases the crowd at potluck dinners.

2 cups sugar
2 cups flour
1-1/2 cups small marshmallows
1/2 cup butter
1/2 cup oil
3 Tablespoon cocoa
1 cup Coke
1 teaspoon baking soda
1/2 cup buttermilk
2 eggs
1 teaspoon vanilla

Preheat oven to 350 (325 for glass pan). Grease a 9 x 13 baking pan. Sift together the flour and sugar, add marshmallows. Stir together and set aside. In a saucepan mix together the butter, oil, Coke, and cocoa. Bring to a boil, then add to the dry mix and blend well. Dissolve the baking soda in the buttermilk just before adding to batter. Add eggs and vanilla, mix well. Bake 45-50 minutes. Test with a toothpick.

While the cake bakes, make the frosting:
1/2 cup butter
3 Tbsp cocoa
6 Tbsp Coke
2 cups powdered sugar
1 tsp vanilla
1 cup chopped pecans

In saucepan, combine butter, cocoa and Coke. Bring
to a boil, then pour over powdered sugar in a bowl and
blend well. Add vanilla and pecans.

Remove cake from oven when done and pour frosting
over it immediately. Cool completely before cutting.

One-Bowl Brownies

These are quick, easy, and rich.
One of my all-time addictions!

4 squares Baker's Unsweetened Baking chocolate
3/4 cup (1-1/2 sticks) butter or margarine
2 cups sugar
3 eggs
1 tsp vanilla
1 cup flour
1 cup chopped pecans or walnuts

Microwave unsweetened chocolate and butter in large microwavable bowl on HIGH for 2 minutes or until butter is melted. Stir until chocolate is completely melted.

Stir in sugar. Add eggs and vanilla; mix well. Add flour and nuts; stir until well blended. Spread into greased 13 x 9 inch baking pan.

Bake at 350° F for 30-35 minutes or until toothpick inserted in center comes out with fudgy crumbs. Do not overbake! Cool in pan. Cut into 24 squares. May drizzle each square with melted semi-sweet chocolate, if desired.

(For cake-like brownies, add 1/2 cup milk with the eggs and vanilla and increase flour to 1-1/2 cups. For high altitude, add another 2 T. flour, as well.)

Classic English Toffee

One of my writing students sent me this recipe. It's so easy and unbelievably good!
It has become a Christmas classic at our house.

1/2 pound real butter
1 cup brown sugar, packed
Several milk chocolate bars
1/2 cup finely chopped nuts

Butter an 8" or 9" square pan, set aside. Unwrap the chocolate bars, chop the nuts, set aside.

In a deep saucepan combine butter and sugar. Cook over medium heat, stirring constantly until mixture reaches 300 degrees (hard crack stage). Immediately pour into buttered pan. Lay chocolate bars evenly over hot candy; when chocolate softens, spread into a smooth layer. Sprinkle nuts over chocolate, press in gently.

Chill until chocolate is firm. Invert candy on a flat surface and break into small pieces. Store in an airtight container.

Cake Mix Cookies

This version came from a Texas friend. I love to make them with those special-flavor seasonal cake mixes, the ones that include a complementary-flavored frosting packet. Yum!

1 15-oz box cake mix* any flavor
1/3 cup butter, softened
1/4 cup shortening
1 egg

Mix all ingredients together, blending well. Drop by teaspoons on a cookie sheet. Bake at 350 degrees 9-12 minutes. Frost with your favorite icing after completely cool.

(*Using an 18 oz cake mix, I added a little vegetable oil to make the dough hold together better)

Sugared Walnuts

This was my grandmother's recipe, a holiday standard at our house. It's now my husband's absolute favorite! (Mine, too, because it's so easy to make. The hardest part is resisting the temptation to stir as it cooks!)

1 cup sugar
5 Tablespoons cold water
1/4 teaspoon salt
1 teaspoon cinnamon
1 teaspoon vanilla
2 cups shelled walnut halves

Combine sugar, water, salt, and cinnamon. Cook over **low** heat to soft ball stage (it takes awhile). **Do not stir.** Remove from heat, add vanilla and nuts. Stir until nuts are well coated. Pour onto waxed paper and gently separate with a fork. Store in an airtight container.

* * *

Thanks for trying our family recipes.
I hope you enjoyed them!

* * *

Visit Connie's website for more recipes
and complete information about her mystery novels.
conneshelton.com